GHOSTS
ALONG THE
TRADEWATER

GHOSTS ALONG THE TRADEWATER

A Collection of
Short Ghost Stories

REBECCA SOLOMON

ISBN: 1490949372
ISBN-13: 978-1490949376

CONTENTS

Foreward   i

The Old Indian   1

The Runner   8

Home Again   13

The Ghostly Party   20

The Darby House Ghost   33

The Red Light Ghost   58

Daddy's Girl   68

The Moonlight Canoe Trip   77

Fairy Hill   86

Old Nettles' Story   106

Magnolia Bluff   115

Voices from the Past   139

FOREWARD

Some of the places in these stories actually exist. Cutoff Farm belonged to my family for almost three generations. It is true that the river flooded and cut off road travel at certain seasons. My grandfather rowed my dad and aunt across in a boat to the road so they could walk to school.

The Darby House is a wonderful old former boarding house in Dawson Springs, KY. It was built in 1886, according to a brochure printed by the Main Street Program, Dawson Springs Chamber of Commerce. It now houses the Chamber of Commerce and the Main Street office, as well as a gift shop. It is in the process of being restored as a period home and is open to the public. Dr. Darby and his daughter, Willie, really existed. As for Willie being a ghostly tenant of the house, you will have to make up your own mind about that. My story is strictly fiction.

Rosedale Cemetery is the largest cemetery in Dawson Springs, and is where most people are interred.

Ole Skool Paranormal and Clifty Creek Restaurant are legitimate businesses.

The Tradewater River flows northward from the Pennyroyal Region of Kentucky and circles Dawson Springs on the north, south, and west. It also borders other towns in other counties before ending its journey into the Ohio River. There are many tall tales about the region around the Tradewater. Some are told for the truth; some, like mine, are made up. But as with any historic place, there are bound to be ghosts...enjoy!

THE OLD INDIAN

At the time of this incident we lived on a wedge of land in Kentucky on the west side of the Tradewater River and bordering Caldwell County. It was a hundred and twenty acres of prime bottom farmland. Our farm was called The Cutoff, because when we got a lot of rain, the Tradewater overflowed its banks and cut us off from the road. We had to go across the flood waters by boat. My dad kept a small rowboat tied to a tree in the bottom of our north pasture for this purpose.

The year was 1900 and I was twelve years old. Dad was going on a trip to Princeton to buy some farm supplies. Ma'am and I would stay at home and take care of the chickens and other chores. "John, I hope you have a safe trip," said Ma'am. "Emmy and I will bake some sugar cookies so you can have a treat when you get back."

Dad smiled as he gave each of us a hug. "That sounds good," he answered. "Emmy's getting to be a right good cook."

"Yes, she is indeed," answered Ma'am. "And she can sew

and quilt pretty well, too." She brushed her fingers through my long dark hair. She started to say something else, but had a fit of coughing.

"Are you all right, Lizzie?" Dad looked worried.

"Oh, yes! Just some dust or something in my throat. Now, don't you worry. Just go on so you can get back."

Dad hitched up our big black horse, old Ben, to the wagon, threw his saddlebags in the back, and climbed up. "I should be home tomorrow evening," he said.

"Bye, Dad!" I called.

Ma'am coughed into her apron as he was driving off. "Let's go in the house, Emmy, and get started on those cookies."

When the cookies were cooling on the counter, Ma'am and I went to the kitchen table by the fire and she darned socks while I worked on a piece of embroidery. I noticed Ma'am's breathing was a little labored, but she just laughed it off when I asked if she was all right.

Suddenly there was a crack of thunder and I noticed the sky outside was dark. The wind had kicked up and was howling around the house. I threw some more sticks on the fire and shivered. It was only April, and I knew the rain would be cold. I wondered if Dad had found shelter for him and Ben. There were plenty of farms between The Cutoff and Princeton and he knew most of the farmers who lived there, so I was certain he would be all right.

I was not so certain about Ma'am, however. Her face was red and she was just sitting and staring and trying to breathe.

"Ma'am, please go and lie down. I'll fix you some tea and maybe the steam will help your breathing," I said.

She nodded and got up, laying her darning aside. I helped her to her bedroom. She took off her skirt and blouse and climbed beneath the homemade quilts. I propped her head up on some pillows so she could breathe easier. She was coughing periodically, but not a productive cough. I didn't like the look of her at all.

I brought the tea and held the cup while she sipped. She wasn't able to breathe deeply enough for the steam to do her much good. She managed to get half the cup down before she lay back, exhausted. "I just feel so weak," she whispered. "I don't know what's wrong."

I was alarmed. Ma'am was the strongest person I knew. It was fearful to think of her being so sick she couldn't sit up. I bathed her face with a cool, wet cloth. Her breathing got worse. She tried to smile at me, but it looked more like a grimace. "My chest hurts some, Emmy. Would you make a mustard and onion poultice and put on me?"

I rushed to do it. Her mother had taught her this remedy for a chest cold. I sliced the onions and spread an old rag with mustard, piled the onions on, with more mustard, warmed it on a griddle on the stove, and slapped it on her chest underneath her chemise.

The rain was coming down in sheets outside when I finally decided I needed to go and get the doctor. Dr. Simson only lived about a mile from us, but on the other side of the river. It had been raining for a good two hours without letup.

"I'm going for the doctor, Ma'am," I said, laying a final cool cloth on her head. I couldn't tell if she heard me. Her breathing was so labored she couldn't answer.   Grabbing an old oil slicker and a felt hat of Dad's, I pulled them on as I stepped out the back door. I could barely see for the sheeting rain. The wind roared like a banshee. I knew there was no point in going toward the road, as the river was bound to be up by now. So I took off across the back pasture, the mud sucking at my shoes. If they had not been laced tightly, I would have lost them in the mire.

I was right. When I got near the tree where Dad always tied up the boat, I saw that it floated on flood waters and was already nearly out of my reach. I waded out a little way and attempted to grab the tree branch the boat was tied to. Normally Dad would have pulled the boat in to dry ground at the first sign of a storm. I made two or three passes, trying not to step any farther into the water, as I wasn't sure how deep it was.

I held onto my hat, which had almost been blown off. I reached one final time and finally grasped the branch. Holding onto it, I worked my way forward. The water was up to my calves and was so cold my teeth chattered.

A chilly fog hung in the air. I shuddered. What if I capsized the boat and drowned? Who would help Ma'am then? I started untying the rope. It was wet and that made it harder. At last the knot came undone. But as I grabbed for the prow of the boat, my hand slipped and the current carried it completely out of my reach. "Drat!" I muttered. I knew better than to try to wade or swim the

4

rapidly flowing waters. Big tears rolled down my cheeks as the boat sailed serenely down the river currents, soon lost to my sight.

About that time, I heard a splash downstream. I peered into the gloom. Around the bend came a canoe, paddled by an ancient Indian (for Native Americans were called that back then). He was dressed in buckskins that appeared to keep him dry. His iron gray hair, pulled back into plaits, seemed to repel the water as well. He did not have a head covering, but seemed unperturbed. His canoe was beautiful white birch bark. He fixed his dark eyes on me and began to paddle towards me.

"Need cross water?" he asked in a deep raspy voice.

I hesitated, but only for a moment. Ma'am needed the doctor, and here was a means of getting him. "Yes, I do! I lost my boat... my ma'am...mother...is very sick and I need Dr. Simson as fast as I can get him."

He reached out his hand to help me into the canoe. His hand was dry and warm. I didn't have time to think about how strange it was, because my only thoughts were for Ma'am and the errand I had to do. When I was seated, he began to paddle across the river; it wasn't far, about a quarter mile. Soon I could see the road.

When we got to the other side, my guide steered the canoe close to the bank, jumped out, and pulled it up so that I could step out on the ground. He helped me out and climbed back into the canoe.

I looked down at my ruined shoes and sagging socks. "Oh, how can I ever thank you enough," I said. When I raised my eyes again, the old Indian was gone. I never even heard the canoe slide back into the water! It was as if he had never been.

The rain and wind had let up some by then. I ran the mile to Dr. Simson's and he hastened to get his doctor's bag and hitch up his horse. Mrs. Simson hovered around me drying my hair with a towel and insisting that I drink a hot cup of sasafrass tea before leaving. I told them the story of how I had lost the boat and gotten across the raging river.

Mrs. Simson looked at me like I had lost my mind. "But, Emmy, there have not been any Indians around these parts for at least 50 years. Are you sure?"

"Of course, I am. But you know, the funny thing was, he didn't seem to be wet, even in the hard rain." I remembered his warm dry hand as he helped me into the canoe. Now that I thought about it, the canoe was not wet, either. I shivered. Had I seen a ghost? Or was it just someone who wanted to visit the old trading grounds? Surely not in weather such as we had that day!

Soon Dr. Simson and I were on our way back down the road. He tied his horse to a tree and threw a tarpaulin over the horse's back to keep off most of the rain. He kept a boat of his own near-by, so we were able to cross the flood. I kept my eyes open, but no sign of the Indian or his canoe was ever seen again. After Ma'am was well enough, I told her the story.

"Did you ever stop and think that sometimes we entertain angels unaware?" she asked me. "Psalm 91:11-12 says, 'For he shall give his angels charge over thee, to keep thee in all thy ways.'

I believe that is what happened in this case. And I am so thankful!" She gathered me in her arms as I whispered my own prayer of thanks for the old Indian.

THE RUNNER

Moonlight on the Tradewater is one of the most beautiful sights I have ever seen, especially on a soft summer night when the mist is rising in the bottoms and the owls are hooting in the woods. The shimmer on the eddies and swirls as they wind their way downstream seems magical, as if the river was sprinkled here and there with fairy dust. The fireflies, or lightning bugs as we always called them, create another kind of magic in the dark of the trees and across the rolling pastures between the river and our house on Cutoff Farm.

Cutoff Farm is a special place; a place that you can not only see but feel. The generations of farm folk that have lived there, as well as the Indians before them who used to camp on the banks of the Tradewater River and meet other tribes as well as white men, for trade, have all left their mark on the place. Not just physically, but in the atmosphere. Maybe that is why so many strange things happen there, such as the one I am about to tell you.

My grandmother, Emmy Thompson Potts, was born and

raised in the house we lived in. She was still alive when I was born. Though getting up in years, she still liked to cook and bake, as well as go cat fishing in the river. She taught me to bait a hook and fish when I was about 6 years old. She also told me some of the history surrounding our farm and some incidents that had happened to her growing up.

Grandma Emmy said that the best time to catch catfish was in the early evening, just when it was getting dark. We had a special place on the riverbank where we would go and fish after supper until it was pitch dark. Then we would light our lantern and bring our fish back to the house, where my dad would clean them and get them ready to cook the next day.

One such evening Grandma Emmy and I sat in our favorite place on the bank. We were fishing and listening to the honk of the bullfrogs and once in awhile a splash as one jumped into the river. The air was warm, but not enough to make you sweat, and the river was casting its spell on us as it chuckled and burbled its way past us.

I became aware of a different sound as I waited for a pull on my line. It was like a steady beating drum, far away. "Grandma Emmy," I whispered. "Do you hear something?"

She put her hand on my arm. "Yes, I hear it. Just sit still until it passes."   Well, the hair on the back of my neck stood up when I realized I was hearing footsteps coming closer along the bank of the Tradewater. It was someone running very fast, and I also became aware of a kind of sobbing breath with each footstep. I looked at Grandma Emmy, what I could see of her face in the dim light. She had a very still, intent look. It was not a frightened look, but more apprehensive.

The running footsteps were almost on top of us now, up the hill behind us a little way. I turned and looked. I saw a shadow of a young girl in a long dress, which she was holding up in the front so she could run. The sobs and hitches of her breath were as clear as could be on the night breeze.

I started to get up. It was obviously someone who needed help of some kind. But Grandma Emmy held onto my arm with a finger on her lips. Then the girl was gone, the sound of her foot-steps fading away in the distance.

Grandma Emmy let out a long sigh and held me close. "What was that?" I asked, incredulous that she had not tried to help the girl. "That was not something we could do anything about. The Runner, I call her. I have seen her many times down here, always running along crying and sobbing, holding up her skirt. What happened to her was a long, long time ago. She is long dead and buried. She can't hurt us, and we can't help her." Grandma looked troubled. "I was hoping you wouldn't ever see her."

I was thoroughly creeped out by now. "You mean, she's a ghost?" I asked softly. I had heard lots of tales from Grandma Emmy, but not this one.

About that time, my line jerked and my attention was taken by landing a good size catfish. But after I had the hook baited again and in the water, I asked Grandma Emmy about the young girl. "I could see her pigtails bobbing and her dress flapping just as plain as anything, even though it was almost dark," I said.

"The way I heard it, there once was a pioneer who built his cabin on the banks of the Tradewater about a couple of miles up from where Cutoff Farm is now. He had a wife and four children, two boys and two girls. I don't know their ages, but they weren't grown. The different tribes of Indians were warring all over Kentucky about that time. The Iroquois were especially fierce and determined to keep all the others out. That included the white men as well. And not many white people had made it into Kentucky yet at that time…this was probably in the late 1700's. Well, this pioneer was determined to take advantage of the rich land and fine timber, as well as the abundant game here, so he moved his family here.

One night when they had been living there about a year, a party of Iroquois attacked the cabin. They were particularly bloodthirsty Indians, according to the history I have read, torturing and burning their victims and making sure they took a long time to die." Grandma Emmy drew in a deep breath, and I shuddered.

The man and his whole family were slaughtered in ways you don't need to hear about. One of the girls escaped. She was about fourteen years old. She had hidden in a trunk and listened to her family being tortured and killed, too afraid even to breathe. When the Indians were done, they set the cabin on fire and rode away. She managed to escape and took off along the riverbank looking for help. There were no other white people for miles, but she eventually came into an encampment of Shawnees who were in Kentucky hunting and trying to avoid the dreaded Iroquois until they could get enough game to feed their families for awhile. The story goes, she fainted dead away when she realized she had run straight into an Indian camp.

But the squaws got her to calm down, signing that they were peaceful people and would not hurt her. She lived with these Indians the rest of her life, eventually marrying one of the chief's sons. When she was very old, there were many white people living along the Tradewater, and different tribes would come to trade hides, beadwork, and moccasins among themselves and with the whites. She was able to tell her story to some of the white people, and tell them who she was. It came out that she had seen her whole family gutted and scalped.

But every year if there is a full moon on the anniversary of her family's deaths, she can be seen running down the old trail. It upsets me more than I can say, what happened to her and her family. But it was so long ago. I always pray for her spirit to find peace."

"And I will too, from now on," I said softly. "But I really hope to never see her again."And from then on I have stayed away from the river bank on a full moon in July.

HOME AGAIN

Tom awoke to the sound of bombs falling and the rattle of anti-aircraft guns. He jumped up, drenched in sweat, his heart pounding, and reached for his M1 Carbine rifle. Not finding it where he expected it to be, which was right by his side, he began to wake up more and finally realized that he was far from southern France. In fact he was home in his own bed in his mother and father's house on a farm in Kentucky on the Tradewater River.

He was dreaming about the war again. He sat up, rubbed his face, took a long breath, and lit a cigarette from the pack on the nightstand. Looking around the familiar room, with the moonlight slanting across the wood floor and the sheer white curtains billowing in the night breeze, he gradually began to calm down as he smoked. He lit another match and looked at his watch. 1:00 a.m. Sighing, he took a last drag and stubbed the cigarette out in the ashtray. He'd not sleep anymore this night.

He had lost several buddies in World War II, good friends that could be depended on. He wondered sometimes why them and not him, but realized that line of thought was not only futile, but detrimental. But when he had these nightmares, they came to him in his memory, joking and horsing around, or grim-faced and aiming their rifles at the enemy.

Tom grabbed his shirt and pants, and slipped his feet into his old shoes. A walk by the river should help clear his head. He crept down the stairs and into the kitchen, being careful not to make any noise that might wake his parents. The screen door creaked a little when he opened it and stepped out onto the back porch.

The full moon lit up the yard and the fields beyond, its silvery light magical and beautiful. He could hear the river before he saw it, as he traced the old path along the bank to his favorite fishing hole. The crickets and frogs set up a lively chorus in the soft June night. He sat down on the bank and tried to empty his mind. He knew he could never forget the killing he had to do and the awful sights that he saw. But he hoped that here in the country, so far away from all the horror, he could start to push it to the back of his mind. He had already made peace with God about it, but it was still hard to forgive himself. Forgive myself, he thought. For what? I did what I had to do.

The answer came to him as tears wet his cheeks. Forgive myself for living when so many others died. Aaron Kinnick's face swam before him; handsome, smiling, always playing practical jokes; but brave and determined in the face of the advance on the Germans until a hand grenade blew him to bits. He was right beside Tom, his blood and brains splattering all over Tom's uniform and hands. That was the wonder of it; that Kinnick got that grenade and Tom was spared. But the unit kept advancing and finally defeated the Germans and captured their position. It was a hollow victory, considering what it had cost.

Tom sat there a long time, thinking about others who didn't come back. He wished he could talk to someone about it, but the thought of sharing all this with his parents was not to be borne. And he didn't intend to go sit in some shrink's office, when it really couldn't change what happened. He thought about his service revolver, all cleaned up, oiled, and ready. It was upstairs in his closet.

In the rush of the water and the intensity of his thoughts, he almost didn't hear the footsteps coming down the old path. A booming voice caused him to turn around. "Sgt. Blackburn! Ten Hut!"

Tom jumped to his feet, astonished to see his old unit leader, 1st Lieutenant Melvin "Melly" Wilkerson, coming down the path, still in his uniform, his cap jauntily set on his head. Melly had been an inspiration to all the men under him, never asking them to do anything he wouldn't do himself. The nickname, "Melly", had been coined because of his last name's resemblance to Ashley Wilkes in Gone With the Wind, and of course, Ashley's wife being Melly, which was conveniently short for Melvin.

Melly looked happy to see Tom and not at all finding it strange to be walking down this particular path at 2:00 in the morning, dressed as if for a full parade inspection. Tom, however, found it very strange, as he was almost sure he had read an obituary for Melly not long after they were shipped back to the states.

He must have been mistaken. "Melly!" he said, and shook his hand. "What on earth are you doing out here?"

"Looking for you, my man," answered the Lieutenant. "I just had a feeling you might need someone to talk to."

Tom gaped. He had not told anyone about his recurring dreams and painful memories. Now he looked Melly up and down. A trim figure in his uniform, his broad, honest face with its straight nose and jutting chin, a wide grin just like he always had. Why was he in uniform? The war had been over for a year.

For some reason, he didn't want to ask. "Sit down here, Melly, and tell me what you've been doing since you came home."

Melly smiled, and sat. He didn't answer Tom's question right away. "I still remember what a good soldier you were, Tom. I remember never having to worry about whether you would be where you were supposed to be, or whether you would do your job. That's something to be proud of. Your country should be grateful to you."

"You're awfully serious, Melly," said Tom, feeling a bit uncomfortable. These were not things men usually said out loud. "You were just as good as me. In fact, one of the best leaders I ever had. And I never got to thank you for the way you helped all of us stay calm in the face of battle. I don't usually talk about these things. Not to anyone. But you were there, and you saw all the dreadful things they did to our boys…you understand."

"Yes, I do. And I had nightmares after I came home, just like you do."

"How do you know that?" Tom asked, staring intently at Melly. "I haven't talked to you since the war, and not to anyone about that."

"I was there, Tom, right along with you and the rest. I saw the things you saw, and experienced the fear, the dirt, and the body parts. You don't have to tell me. It is a pain that never goes away. I know," he said, leaning in close and looking into Tom's eyes. "I know."

Tom looked away, swallowing hard. Of course, Melly knew. "And the shame, Melly? Do you know how ashamed I feel knowing how many of those young Germans will never see their families again because of me? And how I hate myself for being here in this peaceful place while so many of my buddies are never coming home to their parents, wives, and girlfriends?" He got up and paced. "It's all I can think about, why them and not me? Why?"

"It's an answer you won't ever know, Tom," said Melly. "And I know what you are thinking about doing. But I'm going to tell you something you might not have thought about."

Tom was taken aback. How on earth would Melly know how many times he had longed to take his service pistol and put it in his mouth….and have peace? He covered his face with his hands. "What's that, Melly?"

"We were sent over there through no fault of our own to do a job. To save the world, if you will. Of course, we couldn't do it all ourselves. But it had to be done, and thousands of young Americans and young men from the allied countries joined together and got it done! America came late to the war, but come she did, after she was attacked, and helped drive out the evil that threatened our very shores. And some had to die. That was their sacrifice to make sure the world was safe for the ones they loved. Someone had to come back and see that the economy got going again, had to take care of the ones they left behind, and take care of others whose sons and husbands didn't come back." Melly turned his back for a moment.

When he turned back around, he pressed his lips together. "Tom, I felt exactly like you did. I thought if I could just end it all, I'd be at peace. No more bad dreams, no more survivor's guilt." He spread his hands. "But it does not work that way, Tom. A soul goes on and on and on. You realize you took the easy way out. You realize that in the light of that, the enemy has won, every time a soldier takes his own life. You let them have a victory that they don't deserve. Why beat them back only to turn around and hand them back what has been so bravely and determinedly won? Just think about it." Then again, softly, "Just think about it." And he turned and went back up the path.

Tom sat there until first light, thinking on all that Melly had said. It made perfect sense. Tom still had a life to live, and things to do, and his parents needed his help now that they were getting older. His dad was still farming, and he could take a lot of that load off. Tom knew that his burden would never entirely go away, but he decided that when it got particularly rough, he would think about all those men with pride, and try to carry on the job they had passed on to him and his fellow soldiers. Suddenly his heart felt a lot lighter and some of his mom's biscuits sounded really good.

She was already at the stove when he came in the kitchen door. "Out early, I see." She smiled at him.

"I was just walking along the river. It's a special place down there, you know?" He put his arm around her shoulders. "Say, Mom, do you remember my telling you about our squad leader, "Lt. Wilkerson?"

"The one you called Melly? Yes. I do. That was so sad what happened to him. I guess it was just too much for him, what he went through over there."

Tom grabbed a chair from the table and sat down. He could hardly breathe. Melly, out at 2:00 in the morning, in his uniform…. "Yeah, it sure was. But I'll never forget him. Say, Mom, those biscuits sure smell good!"

THE GHOSTLY PARTY

Marian awoke on the riverbank, the quarter moon barely visible, surrounded by a misty ring. Startled, she sat up, tried to look at her watch, but could not make out the time in the darkness. Crickets sang and the river gurgled as it flowed past her grassy spot. It couldn't be dark, could it? Why, she had just gotten here. But she had been so tired, and her eyes were so heavy… Something moved through the bushes to her right and made her jump to her feet. "Crap!" But nothing else happened, and she let out a long breath. Must have been a rabbit or squirrel. What time had she gone to sleep? The moon was pretty high in the sky, so it must have been at least three hours. Marian pushed her long hair back and looked around. It was kind of spooky down here at night, even though it was her favorite place in the daytime. A soft, grassy knoll in a small clearing in the maple and elm trees, it was the perfect place for a dolls' tea party when she was younger, or a fishing spot, or even a secret place where friends could sprawl and throw sticks in the river and talk about life. Marian and her friend, Beth came here a lot before…but she wouldn't think about what happened, not now, when the important thing was getting home before her mother became worried and started looking for her.

Even at fifteen, Marian knew her parents still considered her a child. Sometimes it chafed at her, when she wanted to go to a party or a concert, or stay out past 9:00. She frowned. She was a lot more mature than they thought. After all, she was in love…too bad the boy in question was not aware of it.

She started up the hill to the path, trying not to stumble over a root or rock in the darkness. The woods were alive with sounds; sticks crackling, slithering, calls of nightbirds, and cicadas. Marian turned once more and looked back at the dark Tradewater River, flowing along to wherever it was going. Then she hurried on home. She wished she lived back when Dawson Springs had been a resort, where people came on the train to "take the waters," waters being the mineral water that had been discovered more than a century ago when workmen digging a well had accidentally tapped into it. The mineral water supposedly cured everything from digestive upset to kidney failure, and, it was said, even enabled people in wheelchairs to walk again. Wells soon sprang up all over town.

While the tourists were recuperating, they were treated to all kinds of entertainments; dancing to the music of big bands, live theatre, fine dining, and picnics at The Bluffs, a place down the river a ways. They were taken there by road on horse drawn carriages, or by water on a paddle wheel pleasure boat called the *White City*.

Many a young lady had met her future husband on these excursions. Eagle-eyed mamas saw that their girls had the best clothing, the most fashionable hats and accessories, and were promenaded along the hotel verandas in the evening. It all sounded so romantic! It was a much more exciting life than drudging away in high school, the teachers droning on and on, the rooms smelling like Lysol, and the desks sticky with gum underneath.

Marian's freshman year, which she had so looked forward to, was turning out to be the same old thing as the year before. Maybe this year she would be noticed, be popular! Maybe if she wasn't an A student...maybe if she wore her hair different, or even got it cut short...

One day she talked her mother into putting her hair up into a bun on top of her head. She liked the way it lengthened her neck. Why, I'm almost swan-like, she thought as she turned this way and that in the mirror. But when she got to school, her best friend, Beth, put her hand over her mouth and started giggling. Marian was so embarrassed. "What's wrong with you?" she whispered angrily.

"I'm sorry," Beth said when she got herself under control, "you look like someone from another century!"

"Is that so bad? Maybe I look like one of the water boarders!" said Marian. And she held her head high as she walked down the hall to her first period class. She had forgiven Beth by lunchtime, and as they ate their sandwiches they talked about the water era and how different it must have been.

About that time, Frankie Rossi walked by with his lunch tray. Both girls went silent. Frankie, unaware of how good-looking he was, didn't notice the two girls scrutinizing him. His Italian heritage stood out in his dark wavy hair and brown eyes that sparkled when he talked. He was tall and lean, but muscular. "Can't you just see him in knickers and a celluloid collar?" whispered Beth.

"And twirling a straw hat and carrying a cane?" commented Marian. She had not told Beth how in love with Frankie she was. "He would have been the life of the party on the *White City*! All the girls would have been wild about him. In fact, if I'm not mistaken, his great- grandfather came here in 1896 and ran one of the hotels."

"Wow, Marian, where do you learn this stuff?" Beth's eyes were wide.

In fact, Marian had always been extremely interested in the water era, when the town had boasted over 50 hotels and rooming houses. Her great-grandmother had passed down stories about the exciting times back then. Marian hung on every word of those stories. Her very favorite was about the paddle boat, the *White City*.

A horse drawn taxi would take the guests from the hotels to the river, where they would board the *White City* for a scenic ride down the river a couple of miles to picnic at the Bluffs or just to sightsee on the water.

One particular night the *White City* was loaded down with young men and women who were on a Sunday School outing under the full moon. There was a lot of joking and singing, no doubt distracting the boat operator, who was not watching very carefully. The young ladies in their white dresses and plumed wide hats made a pretty sight as the lighted boat floated down the Tradewater

All of a sudden there was a terrific jolt, and the boat stopped. One young man fell overboard because he was standing up and lost his grip on the post that was attached to the roof. Before the partiers knew what happened, the boat started sinking! They had hit a big rock hidden under the surface of the water. All ten people plus the operator began scrambling for a place to go. But there was none.

Laughter turned to horrified screams, as the girls were plunged into the water, their long full skirts holding them under, making it impossible to swim. Most of them couldn't swim anyway. The boys valiantly tried to save them, and two girls made it to shore held up by their young male friends. Three of the boys made it to shore. The others all drowned, including the boat operator.

Marian's grandmother told her that now, on a full moon, the *White City* comes gliding silently down the Tradewater, and the boys and girls can be seen laughing and singing, but there is no sound. It is all white, in a bluish glow until it comes to the spot where it sank, and then it just disappears. Marian had laughed at the time. But sometimes she wished she could see the ghostly boat with its beautiful young people, just once.

Marian had started wearing her hair down and tied back with a wide ribbon. She decided she liked it better than the bun. One day Frankie Rossi came over and sat at the lunch table with her and Beth.

"Hi," he said, smiling shyly. "Is it okay if I sit here?"

"Sure," said Beth, while Marian gaped like a fish out of water.

"I was just wondering, Marian…" he said. "Someone told me you're practically an expert on the water era in Dawson Springs. My grandfather owned one of the boarding houses. I've been wanting to find out more about him and the time he lived in."

Marian found her voice at last, after looking into his deep brown eyes and nearly swooning. "Well, I don't know if you'd call me an expert." She smoothed her skirt down. "I have read a lot about it, though, and my grandmother tells me stories…"

Frankie grinned. "Well, maybe we could talk about it sometime. Could I come over to your house after school one day?"

Marian about fell off her seat. "A-any day," she managed to croak.

Frankie said, "How about today? I can call my mom from your house and tell her I'll be late. That way I can just walk home with you." He raised his eyebrows. "That is, if you don't have other plans. "

"N-no, I don't. That will be just fine." Marian found herself smiling from ear to ear. Even Beth was smiling.

The first bell rang. They stood and gathered up their trays to dump their trash. "Well," said Frankie." I'll see you at the front door of the school this afternoon. Bye, Beth!"

Marian stared after Frankie as he left the lunchroom. "Am I

dreaming?" she asked.

"Nope, not unless I am, too," said Beth. "Gosh, I wish he'd ask me something like that."

"Well, anybody would wish that," answered Marian. "But, after all, it's not a date. He just wants information."

"But you don't know where it might lead."

"Well, I'm not getting my hopes up. After all, he's the cutest guy in school."

Marian dropped into her seat in English class just as the second bell rang. She never heard a word Mrs. Jepson said as she fantasized about Frankie, the *White City*, and the water era.

Later that afternoon she met up with Frankie at the school door. As they walked toward her house, she was surprised at how easy it was to talk to him, especially about the days when Dawson Springs was a resort. Marian's mother served them cookies and milk while they talked.

Marian was surprised that Frankie had not heard of the *White City*. "I can show you a picture of it!" she exclaimed. She hurried to her room and got the Cenntennial book that had been published when Dawson turned 100. The picture was faded, but plainly showed a group of people on a paddleboat, the women wearing big hats and long skirts, the men in hats, coats, and ties as they leaned on or sat around the white rail that went around the boat.

"Do you know where it sank?" asked Frankie excitedly. "I'd like to see the spot."

"I do! It is a really pretty place. I go there a lot."

"Why don't you ask Beth to come, too?" Frankie asked.

"Ok." Marian answered. She might feel less nervous if Beth came along.

They made arrangements to go there the next day after school. Marian could hardly sleep that night, daydreaming about her and Frankie living in the past, riding on the Tradewater in the *White City*. It was so romantic!

The next afternoon Beth, Marian, and Frankie took the river path to the spot where the *White City* sank. The crickets sang in the weeds as they made their way to the river's edge. The current was pretty fast here. Marian didn't want to get too close to the edge. About that time, Beth flailed her arms and almost fell in. Frankie grabbed her around the waist.

"Hey! Are you ok?" he asked. Beth was white as a sheet.

"Y-yes, I think so. Gosh, that was a close call." She smoothed her blonde hair back from her face. She looked up at Frankie just as he let her go.

"Thanks!" There was no mistaking the hero-worship in her eyes. Marian felt a flare of jealousy.

"You're welcome," said Frankie, looking back at Beth and smiling. Was that admiration Marian saw? She turned away, disgusted. *Get a grip*, she thought. *You're not here on a date. He has no interest in you except history.*

Marian began to tell Frankie and Beth about the hotels and how the *White City* would carry passengers to the picnic grounds and on scenic rides. She also told Frankie about the ghost story, how the boat would come gliding down the river on a full moon night. Frankie asked lots of questions, and she was more than glad to answer, since his full attention seemed to be on her.

"Now, I don't believe in ghosts," said Frankie. "But wouldn't it be fun to come here on the night of the full moon just to see what we could see?"

Beth jumped up from where she had been digging in the dirt with a stick. "Yes! I'm in!" she cried.

Marian frowned. The last thing she wanted to see was Beth and Frankie making calf's eyes over each other in the moonlight. "I don't know…" she began.

Beth gave her a pleading look. "Aw, come on! You're not scared, are you?"

"Of course not! Ghosts can't hurt you, even if they are real. And I don't believe in them anyway. So, okay!"

"Oh, great," said Frankie, "now we just need to look in the almanac and see when the full moon will be this month!"

They found out that the full moon would actually be just three days away, on a Friday night. Marian suggested bringing along some snacks and offered to fix some sandwiches. "I'll bring some cookies," said Beth.

"I'll bring some Cokes in a little cooler," offered Frankie, "and who knows? Maybe we can catch a ride out to the picnic grounds on the *White City*?" He winked at Beth, making Marian jealous once again.

Marian did not tell her mother what they were planning to

do, exactly. She did enlist her mom's help making the sandwiches that night, "for a picnic with Beth and Frankie under the moon to-night."

"Where are you having this picnic?" asked her mother.

"Oh, I don't know yet, probably in Beth's back yard," she answered, crossing her fingers. She felt kind of bad. She had never lied to her mother about where she would be.

Then she got an idea. She called Beth on the phone and said, "Wouldn't it be neat to dress up like the water boarders tonight? We have those long skirts we wore in the centennial celebration last year. What do you say?"

"Oh, that's a neat idea!" exclaimed Beth. "And I'll call Frankie and see if he can come up with something to wear."

"Oh, wow, he'll be stunning!" said Marian.

Suddenly she was excited! Near dark, she put on her long skirt, and a long sleeved blouse that was similar to the ones the ladies wore long ago. She put her hair up in a bun, leaving some tendrils around her face, and admired herself in the mirror. Her dark hair and oval face was quite suitable for the look she wanted. She grinned at herself in the mirror. Not bad at all, she thought.

The three friends met at Beth's house. Beth looked lovely in a long navy blue skirt and flowered blouse, and she had even put on her grandmother's picture hat! Frankie sported a bow tie and a straw hat he had gotten from his dad from last year's centennial.

"Wow! We need a picture of this!" said Beth. She quickly ran to the house and got her mother to come out and make a picture with Beth's camera. Frankie stood in the middle, with his arms around each of the girls' shoulders. Beth's mom captured them for posterity.

The woods were dark and deep, but they kept to the path. The moon was just rising when they arrived at the picnic spot. Frankie set down his cooler and spread a blanket he had brought. There were still a few lightning bugs, though it was getting into the end of September. Their magical twinkling and the silvery light of the moon on the river made for a beautiful scene.

They ate their sandwiches and cookies, all while discussing the water boarders and how life must have been back then. They didn't notice at first that the crickets had stopped singing. But the atmosphere changed without them being aware of it; somehow quieter, and more surreal.

It was Marian who noticed the unearthly glow on the river. She punched Beth with her elbow, as Beth was trying to charm Frankie with smiles and pouts. "What!" whispered Beth.

"Look!" said Frankie all of a sudden, and they turned and looked as the ghostly *White City* rounded the bend and began to float toward them. All three stood up at once. The hairs prickled on the back of Marian's neck.

The boat was bluish white, the revelers clearly visible, laughing and talking and fanning themselves. The women wore large hats, similar to the one Beth had on. The boat operator was busy at the stern, and the paddle wheel turned slowly. The name *White City* was plain to see on the side of the boat. But there was no sound at all. All of a sudden, the ghostly party all turned as one and looked at Marian, Beth, and Frankie on the bank. They pointed and began to beckon to the three, as the boat turned toward the bank. The three friends couldn't hear what the partiers were saying, but their intent was clear. They were going to pick up what they thought were some of their friends who had missed the boat. The young ladies beckoned, their spectral hands reaching out, as the boat neared the bank.

Frankie's mouth hung open. Beth was mesmerized, and actually took a few steps toward the river. Marian had never heard of this happening before. The boat touched the bank, and people began climbing out, and Marian could see right through them! She had such a creepy feeling. She didn't know for a moment what to do. "Th-they can see us!" she said in horror.

It's our clothes! She thought. *They can see us because we are dressed like them!*

"Take off your clothes!" she shouted as one of the women reached to take hold of Beth's hand. Beth and Frankie turned in confusion as Marian stripped off her long skirt and petticoat. Then it seemed to dawn on them. Frankie jerked his hat and tie off, and Beth sailed her hat into the woods and began to take off her skirt. Luckily the girls had worn shorts under their skirts.

As their old fashioned attire vanished, the ghosts began to drift back into the boat. Soon they backed off the bank and promptly disappeared.

"What would have happened if we had not undressed?"

asked Beth.

Frankie, in his boxer shorts, spread his arms and shrugged. Marian looked at her and said, "I don't really want to know."

It was a long time before Marian could bring herself to dream in her favorite spot by the river. She was finally able to get up the nerve. Sometimes Frankie would come with her, but Beth never did. "It was just too creepy," she said. "I never want to see that place again." She even seemed okay with Frankie dating Marian. And Marian was finally happy in her own place and time.

THE DARBY HOUSE GHOST

I have taken some liberty with the house and characters in the next story. The Darby House in Dawson Springs, Kentucky, is real and so are Dr. Darby and his family. Not many personal facts are known about them, and Willie's personality and ambitions are my own invention. The Dawson Springs Main Street Program does have its office there and there is a small gift and craft shop. But I have arranged and furnished the house without being entirely true to the actual rooms and furnishings. The house is similar to what I have described and is worth seeing, as it is a beautiful historic landmark. Ole Skool Paranormal is a real business and Marlon and Marlena Lamb are its owners.

I was greeted by the sounds of hammers banging and the whine of a table saw as I entered the front door of the Darby House. Built in 1886, the year my grandmother was born, it was the oldest house in Dawson Springs, 113 years old. The city had decided to make it into offices for tourism development, and the renovating was in full swing.

"Hello!" I shouted over the din. Receiving no answer, I made my way down the narrow hall to the back room where a man in work clothes was preparing a board for the saw. Before he could start sawing, I said, "Hi, how's it going?"

He turned around, and brushed his hands off on a cloth lying nearby. He stuck out his hand to me and I took it. "Hello, may I help you?" he asked, with a friendly grin. His dark hair looked like he had run his hands through it many times, and his blue eyes flashed between lashes I would kill for. Yes, he was a fine specimen.

"I'm Angie Newcourt. I'll be working here this summer, cataloguing the books and antiques for the city, and overseeing the craft shop. I guess you'd say I'll be the curator. "I cocked my head to one side, enjoying his handsome face.

"Daniel Hamby," he said. "Pleased to meet you. I'm the head contractor on the renovation. My guys and I"-- he paused as a fresh round of hammering from upstairs began. "We're putting up shelves and repairing the old wood around the windows, doors, and fireplaces. We have finished most of the main renovations, just need to do some painting and a few other little things."

"Well, the outside looks great. I'd hate to have to climb up three stories to paint. I'd get dizzy and fall, probably."

"Thanks. And, yes, a lot of people feel that way. I'm lucky heights never bother me. Say, would you like a cold Coke or something? I was thinking about taking a break."

"Sure," I said, shifting my shoulder bag to the other side. "I have had a long drive and could use some refreshment."

Daniel went into the hall and I followed. He led me to a small kitchen on the right side of the house. There was a refrigerator, stove, sink, cabinets, counters, and a table for four. He pulled two Cokes from the refrigerator along with some cheddar cheese cubes in a bag. I sat down at the table while he got crackers from one of the cabinets above the counter and 2 paper plates.

I smiled. "Now, that's what I call service!"

"I aim to please," he quipped, bowing at the waist.

"This is so nice. I am really going to enjoy living here and doing this job."

He raised his eyebrows. "Living here?"

"Yes. They said they had a bedroom fixed up for me and I could just stay here in the house. I will enjoy not having to commute to work."

"Oh, yeah, we did fix up a bedroom with its own bath on the second floor at the end of the hall. I saw some people moving furniture in there last week. I thought maybe it was just part of the staging to make the house look lived in."We finished our snack and Daniel helped me carry my bags into the house and up to the room he had mentioned. It was a beautiful room with old fashioned wallpaper in a green stripe with white flowers that were big enough, but not overwhelming. A white iron bedstead supported a lofty mattress covered in a solid green comforter with large fluffy pillows encased in white pillowcases with crocheted lace and embroidery on the ends. There was a free standing wardrobe and an antique mahogany dresser with nice deep drawers and a wavy mirror. The floors were heart pine with a large beige and green patterned area rug that covered all but the edges of the floor. I peeked in to the modern tile bathroom with its corner shower, roomy vanity, and shiny new commode. "This is gorgeous!" I exclaimed with delight. I went over and looked out through the sheer white curtains at the view behind the house. I could see over most of the city from up here.

Daniel stood in the doorway with one hand on his hip and the other arm on the door facing. "You might not think that if you meet the resident ghost," he said, his eyes crinkling at the corners with a smile.

I whirled around. "A ghost? Why, that's absolutely perfect!" I said. "I should have known a house as old as the Darby House would have one, with all that has gone on within these walls."

"Well, at least you're not a scaredy cat. Come on, I'll show you through the house." He turned and started back down the hall, with me following. He introduced me to Clay and Alex, his two helpers, who were repairing the wood around the doors in the hallway. They nodded as they again picked up their hammers.

The next two rooms were bedrooms, as the Darby House had been a popular boarding house when Dawson Springs was a watering spa with mineral wells and baths, where people at the turn of the century came to restore their health and take part in all the entertainments and amusements in the town. These rooms were also furnished with antique furniture, glassware, and pictures in ornate frames.

The two rooms across the hall from these had not been furnished yet, but were full of boxes and old furniture. I assumed these were some of the items I would be cataloguing. It was going to be a big job. I looked forward to delving into all of the memorabilia, both of the Darby family and also those items which had been donated from people in the community.

We climbed the narrow stairs to the attic. "Be careful up here," Daniel warned. "We haven't really done much and the floor is uneven." He pulled on a string that hung down from an old fashioned light bulb fixture and the place lit up. I noticed the light didn't quite reach all the corners. I looked toward the two front windows, where daylight palely made its way in.

I looked out one of the windows and could see City Hall across the street. "That's the window the ghost has been seen in," remarked Daniel.

Suddenly I felt a little cold. "I certainly hope no one below mistakes me for it," I said, trying to laugh. I rubbed my hands together briskly. "Well, shall we go back to the first floor? I can unpack my stuff later. I want to take a look at the craft shop."

We made our way back down the stairs, and I held tightly to the rails, as they were very steep. Daniel turned into the first room on the left at the bottom of the stairs. It was large and airy, with lace curtains. Glass fronted merchandise cases filled the room waiting for the crafts that would soon be on display. Some were here already, I noticed, admiring the wood carvings and knitted scarves someone had laid out. A few watercolor paintings of the local scenery hung on the walls. A big wood sign hung in back of the counter that ran along the west wall. "KENTUCKY CRAFTS

AND GIFTS" had been woodburned into it and the letters painted black.

I lifted the lid on a cardboard box and took out a bright red T-shirt that said "Dawson Springs" with "A Very Special Place" underneath it. "Oh, I've gotta have one of these," I said, smiling at Daniel. He smiled back.

"Do you know who will actually be working in the craft shop while I am doing the cataloguing?" I asked.

"Yes, in fact, she happens to be my sister Caroline. She is coming in this afternoon to do some more unpacking."

"That's great! I'll look forward to meeting her. "

"Well, I'd better get back to work on your office. Soon as I get those shelves up, you can start moving and arranging whatever you are going to put in there." And with a wink, he was off down the hall, leaving me to wander across to the other front room, which was furnished as a parlor.

A large horsehair sofa and matching chair stood along one side with a little tea table between them. A large grandfather clock stood in one corner. There was also a little sewing rocker and a large wicker planter with an artificial fern in it. Over the large fireplace hung a portrait of Dr. A.G Darby, who had built the house, according to a small plaque underneath the picture. The walls were done in another antique style print, blue background with pink flowers this time. More white lace curtains graced the tall windows On the wall over the sofa was a portrait of a young woman with long hair tied back with a ribbon. She was looking to the side, very serious, with a firm looking chin. She was not beautiful, but what I would call striking. A force to be reckoned with, I thought. The plaque proclaimed that this was Dr. Darby's daughter, Willie.

Another plaque on one of the walls explained that after Dr. Darby's death in 1918, Mrs. Darby, their son Frank, and daughter Willie ran a boarding house there to make ends meet. Mrs. Darby's picture was on another wall, but there was no picture of Frank.

I went on to the other rooms in that hall, which consisted of a sitting room and one outfitted as a doctor's office, even though I knew from my contacts at the city that they were not really sure which rooms the doctor had actually used. Across the hall from that was an empty room that had not been furnished yet, even though it bore a new coat of light yellow paint. Next was the small kitchen, and back of that and across the whole back of the house was my light filled office, where I looked forward to setting up my computer and my shelves of books and reference materials that I was having shipped from my home in Lexington. I could hear the shelves being nailed in place, so I didn't go back there.

Caroline proved to be a lively, vivacious blonde 19 year old who was working for the summer before she went off to college. I took to her immediately. We spent the afternoon unpacking the boxes and crates for the craft shop and a few craftspeople from the area dropped off some of their wares for sale. By the time 5:00 rolled around, we had the place looking pretty good, with T-shirts on racks, crafting books, and other things on shelves and in the cases.

"This looks great!" said Caroline, as she dusted off her hands and picked up her purse. "Say, where are you eating dinner?"

"I hadn't even thought about it," I admitted. "Do you know somewhere good but cheap?"

"Of course I do! College girls know cheap if anyone does. And the best food around is at Dilly's Diner. It's just down the street."

"Would you join me?" I asked her as we walked out to our cars.

"Don't mind if I do," she grinned, and said, "We can take my car and I'll drop you off back here."

We had a great meal, and she was right about it being good. As I leaned back and patted my stomach, Caroline leaned close and whispered, "Did Dan tell you about the ghost?"

"Yes, as a matter of fact. I am thrilled! And I'd like to know more about it."

"Well, some think it is the doctor's daughter. This ghost hunting team went in there a few months ago and got some audio and some weird pictures. It appears to be her looking out of windows, etc. I wouldn't be so thrilled to sleep in that house." She shuddered, but I could see the twinkle in her blue eyes, so much like Daniel's.

When we got back I realized that I had not left so much as a night light on and it was good and dark on the front porch of the Darby House. I unlocked the door and reached for the light switch by the front door. The porch light came on, and the other switch illuminated the long hallway. I sighed in relief. I would not have wanted to negotiate those stairs in the dark. I said goodnight to Caroline and closed and locked myself in. I went to check the back door, which was off the kitchen in a little closed in porch area, turning on lights as I went. It was secure, so I turned off the kitchen light and started back down the hall.

As I got to the foot of the stairs, I thought I heard a noise in the front parlor. I stopped and listened. It did not come again, so I continued up the stairs, first turning on the light at the bottom. Luckily there was a switch at the top and the bottom of each stairway. You're letting this ghost talk get to you, I thought as I reached my bedroom. I really didn't believe in ghosts, and was looking forward to debunking the whole thing.

I took a hot shower in my little bathroom and dug out a pair of pajamas from my small suitcase. The rest of the unpacking could wait until tomorrow. I was tired.

Setting my cell phone next to my bed, I lay down and pulled the fresh smelling sheets up over me. Gosh, it felt good to lie down. It took me awhile to go to sleep, because I was excited about my upcoming work and also a little about Daniel, truth be told.

I slept like a log, and if any ghosts walked, I never heard them. I awoke to a beautiful day and birds singing outside in a tree by my window. I raised the window and leaned out. They had not put screens in yet up here, though they had them downstairs. I could see Daniel's truck pulling into the parking lot below. I'd better get dressed!

I opened my big suitcase and began taking out clothes and laying them on the bed. I found a pair of denim capris and a white T-shirt and put them on with sandals. Hurriedly I brushed my shoulder length brown hair and put on a headband.

Clattering down the steps, I almost barreled into Daniel, who put out a hand to steady me. "Oops, I'm sorry," I said, embarrassed.

He gave me a wide smile. "I'm not," he said. He stepped aside and said, "After you."

I went on downstairs into the kitchen. Instead of going upstairs, he followed me. "I was hoping you'd be up. I brought breakfast."

"Oh, you didn't have to do that," I said, but was pleased that he had, as I had not laid in any groceries yet.

He proceeded to the counter, where several sacks were sitting and pulled out sausage biscuits and doughnuts, several kinds, in fact. He got a coffee maker and coffee down from the cabinet and made a pot of the most delicious coffee I had ever tasted. We ate at the table and talked about the house and the work that had been done. Then he asked me about myself and I told him how I had graduated college last year with a degree in Art History, which everyone knows is useless (he laughed at that), and that I had lived with my mom in Lexington, but jumped at the chance to take this job. It was probably the nearest thing I could get to my field. My mom knew the mayor of Dawson Springs and that is how I had found out about it.

He told me he owned his own construction company, had started out with his dad, but they couldn't see eye to eye, so after learning all he could, he had struck out on his own and was doing pretty well. "Construction and home repair—there's always a market for them. I get a lot of business in the summer, and then in the winter, I just go skiing or something, whatever I decide to do."

"That sounds like a good life to me," I said.

Finally he got up and said, "I've got to go to work now and stain those shelves in your office. Say, would you want to have dinner with me tonight?" He looked like he was afraid I'd say no.

I kept from laughing. "Of course. What time?"

"Well, I'm not sure exactly what time we will be done here. I'll holler at you when we finish up, how's that?"

"Great." I felt fluttery inside, but tried not to show it. I gave him a small wave as he went down the hall, where the other guys had just come in.

That night we ate at Clifty Creek Restaurant, at the nearby state park. We had a table in the rear of the rustic dining room, over-looking the lake. It was a beautiful evening. I found Daniel incredibly easy to talk to, and before long, the subject turned to the Darby House ghost.

"I have to admit, I am very interested in this ghost, even though I don't believe in them. How do you think these stories got started?" I asked him.

"Actually, people that have been working to furnish the house have heard and seen some unexplained things. So they got a paranormal investigative team to come in and see what they could find. And, actually, they got some very interesting pictures. I haven't seen them, myself, but they say the doctor's daughter, or someone very like her, stands in the attic window on the left, as I told you that first day. There is also one of her, or someone, looking in the basement window from outside."

I was really intrigued now. "I'd like to get a look at those pictures," I said, laying down my napkin. "But right now, I'd like some Derby pie." I smiled.

Daniel smiled right back. My heart flipped. He was so nice to look at.

"I think that can be arranged," he answered, signaling for the waitress. "And, I think we could probably look at the pictures on the paranormal team's website. I'd like to see them, too."

When we arrived back at the Darby House, I unlocked the door and we headed for the kitchen, where my laptop sat on the table. I booted it up, and soon we were looking at the pictures that Ole Skool Paranormal had posted. As with most ghost pictures, it was hard to tell what you were looking at. Could it be a reflection that looked so much like a person looking out the window? As for the basement pictures, I couldn't tell anything about them. I stared as hard as I could, but for the life of me, could not see anyone.

"I can't tell for sure," said Daniel.

"Me, neither," I said. "You can sort of make out a person, but then you think, is it my imagination?"

We tried to get closer to the screen to look at the attic picture. About that time, somewhere in the house, a clock began to strike. We both jumped. We froze until the clock had chimed nine times. "Geez," said Daniel.

We began to laugh. "It's that darn grandfather clock in the parlor. I didn't know anyone had wound it! Gosh, I can't believe how jumpy we are!"

I shut the laptop and we made our way to the front parlor. The grandfather clock sat in its corner, as usual, but it was not running. The pendulum hung perfectly straight and still. No ticks could be heard. Daniel and I looked at each other.

"Ok, this is getting totally weird," I said.

Daniel crossed his arms. "Something had to have jarred it."

"What? We would have heard or felt it. This house is solid as a rock."

I felt jittery. I needed air. "Let's go outside," I said, grabbing his hand. His big warm fingers closed around mine, and I felt jittery for a different reason.

Once on the porch, I breathed deeply of the soft night air. We sat down in two large rockers.

"Angie, are you afraid to sleep here? Because I know my sister would…"

I turned to face him. "No, I'm not afraid. I'm going to try and get to the bottom of this whole thing. I'd like to talk to that paranormal team, find out just what they experienced here. There has to be a natural explanation."

Daniel scratched his head. "Well, they're located here in town. Let's see what we can find out. Because I'm getting interested myself."

We made our way back into the kitchen, opened up the laptop, and soon found the address and phone number of Ole Skool Paranormal. It was too late to call, but we decided that I would give them a call first thing the next day.

Daniel gave me a long, warm kiss at the front door when he left, and I practically floated up the stairs. The last thing on my mind was the ghost, as I drifted into a peaceful sleep.

As I still had not had time to go to the grocery store, I went out the next morning and had an excellent breakfast at Dilly's Diner. Afterward I stocked up on staples at the local IGA. When I returned to the Darby House, Caroline was already in the gift shop putting out more inventory. After storing my groceries in the kitchen, I flew in to help her, and we spent a pleasant couple of hours arranging ornaments, T-shirts, and books, as well as getting to know each other better. Before I knew it, it was lunch time.

I fixed myself a turkey sandwich and pulled out the notepad Daniel had written the phone number on last night. I ate my sandwich and had a glass of milk. Then I called Ole Skool Paranormal.

I explained who I was to Marlon Lamb, the owner, and asked if he could come over and talk to me about their investigation into the Darby House ghost.

"Sure, I'll be glad to," he said. "And I'll bring my laptop with all my pictures on it."

We made arrangements to meet that night after closing and dinner. While I waited for him, I walked out near the road where I could see the attic. Looking up, I caught my breath. Though it wasn't dark yet, it looked like someone was just turning and leaving the window. It wasn't there but a second, but I felt like I had just missed them. Goosebumps broke out on my arms. I was still staring up there when a car pulled into the parking lot at the side.

I saw a middle aged man with graying hair getting out. A pleasant looking lady was with him. They didn't look like my idea of ghost hunters.

"Hello, I'm Angie Newcourt," I said. "I'm so glad you could come."

"Marlon Lamb," he said, shaking my hand. "And this is my wife, Melena."

"So nice to meet you," I said, shaking her hand as well.

We sat down in the front porch rockers. Marlon moved a potted plant off a table and sat his laptop on it. "So, are you having some experiences?" he asked.

"I'm not sure. A couple of things. But I think there is a natural explanation for them. I'd like to hear your take on it." I told him about how I had thought I'd seen someone leaving the window just as they drove up.

"Well, as you know, we have investigated this house before. We have seen a woman that we believe to be the doctor's daughter. I think she is stuck here for some reason. No one knows much about her or any of the Darbys. We have tried to communicate with her, but didn't get any vocal response."

I leaned forward. "What do you mean, no vocal response? Did you get some other kind of response?"

Melena chimed in. "We heard noises in the front parlor, like furniture being moved around. But of course, when we went in, there was no one there. It felt cold in there, though. Marlon's thermometer showed it was 40 degrees, and it was summer. As we stood there, asking if someone was with us and wanted to talk, the grandfather clock began to chime. After that, the temperature warmed up."

I gaped at her. "Not only did I hear noises in the parlor the other night, just last night Daniel Hamby and I were here and that clock chimed! But it was not running when we went to check."

They looked at each other. "Sounds like the spirit is getting more active," said Marlon. "She must want to communicate something, for sure. We should set up again and try to get more information. I'll contact the city clerk's office and get permission to come back with our equipment, if that's all right with you."

"Oh, yes, please! I want to find out what is going on. But I'll tell you right now, I don't believe in ghosts."

Marlon smiled and nodded. "I understand. But I won't say any more until we see what we can find out."

"Thank you," I said.

"I have pictures here that we took on our last investigation here," he said, pointing to the laptop. "Have you seen them?"

"I have," I said. "But let me look at them again and you tell me exactly what we are seeing."

So he pointed out the ghostly appearances of someone in the windows. I could see something with his description, but still was not convinced it was Willie Darby, or a ghost at all.

"Well, I'll keep an open mind," I finally said. "I am anxious to see what you find the second time."

Marlon closed the laptop and promised to be back the next evening if the city gave him permission. I watched them drive away, feeling a little uneasy. What was really going on here?

Daniel and his crew were putting the finishing touches on the upstairs rooms. They would soon be through and I wouldn't be seeing his smiling face every morning. I wondered if he would still ask me out. I had not felt this way about anyone in a long time.

I thought about confiding in Caroline, but decided against it. I didn't know that she would keep it to herself. Though I liked her very much, I was wary of trusting too soon. We had the gift shop ready to open. The city had given her money for the cash register, and hopefully tourists visiting the nearby Tradewater River and the state park would be pouring in. We were set to open in two days, which would be on a Monday. I didn't imagine we would have a big crowd that day, but it would get our feet wet, so to speak.

I spent the day cataloguing antiques in the downstairs rooms, dusting the furniture as I went. I wanted everything to be perfect when we opened the house to the public. I found myself standing in front of the picture of Willie Darby. 'What are you thinking?' I wondered. 'Do you have unfinished business here? I wish I knew.'

That night I turned off all the lights and started up the stairs. The air felt thick in a way I can't describe. The night light in the hall by my room flickered. Just as I got nearly to the top of the stairs, I stumbled and the light went out. I grabbed for the hand rail, but missed. Throwing out my arm so suddenly unbalanced me.

My last thought before I sailed backwards was 'Why didn't I bring a flashlight?' and then everything went black.

I awoke in a dim whitish light. A dark haired woman was bending over me with a look of concern. I hurt all over, but especially my head. I felt my forehead. My hand came away sticky. I was bleeding! I must have blacked out again, because the next time I woke up it was daylight and someone was turning the key in the front door.

And then Daniel and Caroline were there. "Angie! Angie, are you all right? What happened?" he cried. He told Caroline to call 911. As she dashed for the phone in the gift shop, I moaned. It hurt to move.

"I think I'm ok, but I'm not sure." Daniel looked me over and felt my arms and legs for broken bones. Not finding any serious injuries, he helped me sit up.

"What did you do to your head?" he asked.

"I must have hit it when I fell. It's bleeding! I'll bet my face is a mess."

He looked at me strangely. "But there's a bandage on it. You must have done it before you fell. There's no blood at all."

I put my hand to my head. Sure enough, I felt gauze and some kind of funny tape. The dark haired woman! It all came rushing back. I could feel myself turning pale.

Daniel put his arm around me to keep me from falling back. About that time the paramedics came in the door. They examined me thoroughly and I refused to go to the hospital. "I'll be all right.

Just sore, is all." They finally left, after telling me to be sure and call if I felt worse or developed a severe headache.

"Don't let her go to sleep for several hours, in case she has a concussion," one of them warned Daniel.

"Don't worry, I'll watch her closely," he said.

When I was finally able to stand, I told Daniel and Caroline all about what happened, including the woman who had obviously bandaged my head. I was afraid to say it had looked just like Willie Darby.

They were surprised, or maybe flabbergasted was a better word. That's how I felt, anyway. We went into the front parlor and sat on the old fashioned sofa. "It had to be the doctor's daughter," said Caroline. "She must be a powerful ghost to be able to manifest in such a concrete way. That is very unusual. She probably helped her father in his practice; that's why she knew how to bandage your forehead."

It was hard for me to say I didn't believe in ghosts in light of all that had happened. Where did the gauze come from? Then I remembered the doctor's cabinet in the room we assumed was his office. There was gauze and tape in there. I sat back, exhausted.

"Are you sure you are ok? I'll get you some water," offered Caroline.

"That would be good."

When she had left, Daniel hugged me and looked into my eyes. "I was so scared when I looked in the door and saw you on the floor," he said. His eyes actually teared up. Then he was kissing me like there was no tomorrow.

I became aware of someone clearing their throat. When we looked up, Caroline was standing there with the water, grinning from ear to ear. "That ought to cure what ails you," was her quip as she surveyed the situation.

I could feel my face getting red. I looked at Daniel. He was starting to laugh. "Maybe I should take up the medical profession if that's the case," he said.

Then we were all laughing. I hoped I would always have these two in my life.

After making me promise to lie down for awhile, Daniel went out to his truck to get his tools. From my bed, I could hear him and his crew, who had arrived after all the excitement. Caroline came up to check on me several times to keep me awake. She had brought her IPod so I could listen to music, along with a bottle of Ibuprofen for my pain.

"I was hoping you and Daniel would get together," she said when she brought up a tray with a sandwich and a cup of tea. "He needs someone, and he is a really good guy."

I smiled at her. "I'm sure of that. I liked him from the start."

"But this ghost business...I don't like it. Aren't you afraid to sleep here?"

"Well, if it is Willie, she sure doesn't mean to harm me. My fall was just an accident."

Caroline bit her lip. "You know, I read that Willie really wanted to take over her father's practice when he died. But back then it was very difficult for a woman to be a doctor, and there was no money for medical school. So she just had to be content with helping her mother run the boarding house. Maybe she is trying to fulfill her wish by taking care of people."

"Are you indicating that she may have caused my fall so she could treat me?"

Caroline looked away. "I didn't say that."

"That's a big leap. Besides, I remember stumbling because the light went out…"

We looked at each other. "No, no, I refuse to believe that."

Caroline shrugged. Picking up the tray, she admonished me to try to get some rest. "It's been over three hours now so you can probably take a nap."

I drifted off soon after that, in spite of the cascading thoughts in my mind. I remembered that Marlon and his ghost hunting team was supposed to come that night, and hoped they could shed some light on what was happening. Maybe they could figure out how to send Willie on to where she needed to go.

Melena called me later in the day and woke me to tell me they would be there that night with all their equipment. I told her what happened and she expressed concern for me before we hung up. "The activity is definitely escalating," she said. "I'll bet we get some pictures tonight, and hopefully some audio. If we can communicate with the spirit, perhaps we can find out what she wants."

That night the Lambs arrived and set up thermal scanners, cameras, and EVP recorders in the house from attic to basement. There was also other equipment for registering magnetic fields and changes in the light. I was still sore, so I opted to sit on the front porch while they roamed the house trying to communicate with the spirit. I wasn't sure I wanted another face to face encounter with Willie Darby, if that's who it was.

I left the porch light off, because I didn't want to draw bugs and mosquitoes. It was quite dark where I sat in the rocker. About midnight, I must have dozed off. I became aware of a slight creaking noise close by. I slowly opened my eyes and looked around. The rocker on the other side of the little table was rocking. Thinking someone had just gotten up, I whispered, "Melena? Marlon?" There was no answer.

The rocker kept on rocking. The hair on my arms stood straight up. "Willie?" I ventured. The rocker stopped. I was shivering now. "There are no such things as ghosts," I whispered to reassure myself. Suddenly the little table was flung over, the potted plant falling to the porch floor and breaking.

Marlon rushed through the front door. "What happened?" he asked.

I gestured to the overturned table. I couldn't find words to tell him. He looked at the dial on the machine he was carrying. "It's going wild! Melena!"

She came through the door and looked at what he had. "There is definitely someone here," she said. "Can you hear us? Can we help you? "We all looked around, waiting for an answer.

The grandfather clock in the parlor began to strike. So we

moved into the house and I said, "I think I offended her. I whispered that I didn't believe in ghosts and that's when the table fell over."

"Well, she certainly has shown that she is real," said Marlon. "Willie? Is that you? What can we do for you? Can you tell us or show us?"

About that time something crashed in a room down the hall. We hurried along the hall to the doctor's office. The cabinet with the old medicine bottles was on its side on the floor.

"It's something to do with medicine and doctoring," I said. I told them about Caroline's theory that Willie had been thwarted in her desire to be a doctor.

As soon as I said that, a sigh floated through the air. We all looked around the room. "I think we all heard that," said Melena.

"I have an idea, but you may think it's silly," I said.

"Tell us, "said Marlon.

"Well, I know Willie can never be a doctor per se. But I know she was almost certain to have helped her father. She has shown what she can do by bandaging my head. And I'm sure that's not all she can do. What if we just gave her the credit she deserves? Maybe then she could move on."

They liked that idea.

The next day was Daniel's last day to work. I told him all about the night before over breakfast of sausage and biscuits that he had brought from Dilly's Diner. He was astounded. He also thought it was a good idea to incorporate more about Willie into the exhibits in the house, especially the doctor's office.

So Caroline and I moved her picture into the doctor's office. I set up a small table in there and made some signs on the computer to put under her picture and on the table and suggested things she probably did to help her father. "I'll bet he taught her most of what he knew," said Caroline.

"It sounds logical. Who knows how many patients were saved because of her help?" I said. "I'm going to do a brochure on women doctors from that era. People should know that Willie would have made a fine doctor; I guess you could say was a fine doctor."

The Lambs came by that evening to show me their evidence. "This is the best stuff we have ever gotten," Marlon said. "This will cement our credibility in the ghost hunting world. "

He had an audio recording of the ghostly sigh, and several pictures of the hall and the parlor where we could see a dark shape in different spots. The camera in the doctor's office actually showed the cabinet falling over and no one there.

Daniel showed up as they were leaving, as he had asked me out to dinner that night. They all shook hands and Daniel said, "I sure hope this is the end of the ghostly stuff. I hate to have Angie alone here."

"But I'm not alone," I said. "Dr. Willie Darby is watching out for me." We all felt the soft breeze across the porch. I smiled.

"Well, I am hoping for more company for you than Dr. Willie," said Daniel, then, catching himself, "not that there's anything wrong with that!"

We all laughed. "Well, we've got to go. Have a nice evening, and thank you, Angie," said Melena.

Daniel and I stood arm in arm as they walked to their car and drove off. I looked up at him. He had a twinkle in his deep blue eyes. "I wonder how Dr. Willie would feel about sharing you with me. I mean, on a permanent basis."

I blinked. "Oh, I think she'd be delighted," I said, as he took me in his arms.

THE RED LIGHT GHOST

Deep in the woods up in Christian County where the Tradewater River starts, there is a place that hardly no one goes. My friend Ed grew up there on a farm near this place, but it wasn't on their land. He and his dad used to coon hunt back in the woods all around and he had been through there, but never liked it. He said it gave him a creepy feeling, and they avoided it if possible. But once in awhile the dogs would run in that direction in the black night, baying at the top of their lungs as they chased a coon clear to Bryant's Hill up toward Latham Road.

Ed loved tramping through the woods with his dad carrying their old shotguns. His dad had told him that legend had it that at a certain place in these tangled trees and weeds a man had driven his car deep into the woods and either shot himself or someone had shot him. The case had really never been solved. It wasn't as grown up out here then; it was years and years ago. But at night if you were in the right place at the right time, you could see the red glow of his brake lights through the trees. And if you hung around, you might hear someone getting out of the car and slamming the door, then the heavy tread of footsteps coming toward you through the dead leaves on the ground.

Ed had laughed when he heard it. But he noticed that his dad always walked around a certain place out there where the trees were thick and and the hoot owls made their spooky cry. "Why don't we just cut straight across, Dad?" he had asked one night when the dogs were making their music. "We'll never catch up with those dogs."

"Sure we will. We need the exercise. Come on." And he started off, expecting Ed to follow, which he did.

Soon they came to the tree where the dogs were baying and jumping all around its base. "Whooee, got one treed!" said his dad. "Good dogs, good dogs." Ed held the light while his dad shot the coon out of the tree.

The dogs ran back and forth, their tongues lolling, panting and smiling. They knew they had done a good job. Ed patted them "Way to go, Old Dan, good girl, Ethel. Good boy, Sambo." It tickled him to see how they knew what was expected of them and how they enjoyed the praise afterwards.

His dad put the coon in a knapsack and came over and praised the dogs all over again. "Let's go home and show Mom what we got," he said.

Ed didn't start walking right away. He thought before asking his dad his question. It had been rolling around in his mind all night. "Dad?"

His dad stopped and turned around. "What, son?"

"Dad, that place you went around instead of going through. Is that where that man—you know, that man that drove his car out here…"

"So they say. Now, I don't believe in the red light nonsense," he said, looking Ed straight in the eye. "I ain't never seen anything in there. I just don't care anything about going through there, is all. The dogs do sometimes, and they ain't bothered. There ain't nothing there. I like to walk, and don't see no reason to go through a bunch of brambles, that's all. Now, let's go home."

"Yes, sir," said Ed.

Ed forgot about their conversation soon after that. Summer in the country was a busy time. He was busy helping his dad on the farm and doing chores for his mom. Sometimes in the evening I would go over there and we'd throw an old baseball around.

One such evening we were sitting on his front porch with glasses of iced tea and some homemade cookies his mom had brought out. "Champie," said Ed, "tonight is supposed to be a full moon. Sure would be a great night to go coon hunting. But Dad has a meeting in town tonight. How about you going with me?"

"I'd love it! But I don't have a shotgun. You know my mom won't allow it." My dad had been killed in the coal mines and Mom was raising me by herself. I felt that she was a little bit over-protective.

"That's ok," said Ed. "You can hold the spotlight. It'll be fun tramping through the woods and all. And you can just spend the night. I already asked Mom and Dad."

"Ok," I said. "I'll just call Mom and let her know." This was perfect. Spending the night with Ed was something I did from time to time. Mom didn't have to know we'd be alone in the woods with a shotgun. I'd just leave that part out.

Sure enough, Mom said it was all right and Ed and I were soon getting the dogs out of their kennels and leashing them up. Ed had been hunting with his father so much that he was allowed to take the dogs out because his father knew he would always bring them home and he was responsible for a fifteen year old. And gun safety had been drilled into him from the time he was a little kid.

We walked across the big field behind the barn. It was almost dark already, and the fireflies were out in droves under the purple sky. It looked dark in the woods, but after we entered the tree line we could still see pretty good. A little ways in, Ed unhooked the dogs' leashes and said, "Go get us a coon, boys and girls!" They took off at a fast trot, their noses to the ground.

Ed and I kept walking in the general direction the dogs had gone. It smelled like pine and earth in here, and though it was a hot night, there was a little breeze that cooled our faces. I loved it. It wasn't long until far off we heard the dogs in full cry. "Let's go, Champie!" said Ed. We were both excited as we took off, being careful not to trip over any roots or logs. Ed knew these woods like the back of his hand, so we were in no danger of being lost.

We kept moving as fast as we could, while the dogs' voices seemed to get no closer. Finally, we seemed to be drawing nearer to the racket when Ed suddenly stopped. He rubbed his chin. "What's wrong?" I asked.

I didn't know it, but we were at the place where the red light supposedly appeared through the trees. "Champie, we could cut right through this brush and stuff here and get to where the dogs are a lot quicker. But I want to tell you, this is the place where the red light appears." He turned to me. "I ain't never seen it, mind you. But if you're scared..."

I was a little scared, but wasn't going to let on. "Naw, let's go," I answered.

So we pushed our way into the grown-up weeds and bushes, Ed holding his shotgun high, sometimes using it to clear the way. The crickets were loud in here, and I heard a whippoorwill somewhere. We were making a mighty lot of noise as we kept beating back the bushes. So we never noticed when it got quiet until Ed stopped to wipe sweat off of his face. Being behind him, I had to stop, too. There was no sound...no crickets or night birds, and even the breeze had died. We could still hear the dogs, but they sounded really far off. The hot blackness pressed in upon us.

Gradually I became aware of a creepy feeling. I strained to see ahead, hoping we would soon be clear of this thicket. It was then, as Ed took a deep breath, then gasped, that I saw the faint red glow up ahead about 300 yards. It pulsed a few times, like someone pumping the brakes on a car. We didn't wait for the sound of the car door slamming. We turned tail and ran as fast as we could and Ed was saying, "Oh, crap! Oh, crap! Oh, crap!"

I was too out of breath to say anything myself, trying to keep up and also not trip over anything. We ran all the way back out of the woods. It was on the edge of the field that we realized that we had left both the shotgun and the dogs in the woods!

"Did you see it, Champie?" whispered Ed.

I nodded my head rapidly. "I sure did! But what are we going to do now?"

Ed wiped his hand over his mouth and chin. "I never thought it was real. Do you think we imagined it?"

"How could we both imagine something at the same time?" I asked.

"Oh, me! I've got to get that shotgun back or my dad will kill me."

"What about the dogs? Will they come back home?"

"I don't know, we have always brought 'em back. I've got to go back in there." He shuddered.

"Now?" I asked, knowing the answer.

"Yes, now, I can't leave those dogs out there."

So we turned and started back towards the woods. When we reached the thicket, we saw the shotgun lying on the ground where Ed had dropped it in his haste to get away from the Red Light Ghost. He picked it up. "I'm glad we don't have to go in there looking for it."

Then he began to call his dogs, as we skirted the thicket. I knew it was at least a mile until we were past it, and I was shaking in my boots.

"Old Dan! Ethel! Sambo! Come! Come on!" We couldn't hear any baying or barking at all now.

"Whoooooeeeee!" Ed cried. "Come, dogs, come!"

"Not so loud," I whispered.

"How else are they gonna hear me?" He spread his hands and shook his head.

I was hoping we had seen the last of the red light. We tramped on through the weeds in the dark, shining our spotlight ahead of us. Ed kept calling the dogs, and finally Ethel came bouncing up to him, tail wagging, tongue out. She seemed to be saying, 'What happened to you? Where have you been?'

Ed patted her on the head. "Good dog, good dog. Now where could your brothers be?" After snapping Ethel's leash on, we kept on walking. I couldn't help but look to my left, into the thicket where we had seen the red light.

Just as we heard the other dogs barking up ahead, another sound reached us. It sounded just like the sound of a car door! Ed stopped and handed me the light. He raised his shotgun and waited. Were those crackling noises in the woods footsteps or something else? Some night creature? Maybe a deer? I was holding my breath as it got nearer.

Suddenly the other two dogs bounded out of the woods and ran towards us. We both let out sighs of relief. Ed quickly snapped on their leashes and said, "Let's get outta here."

It seemed as if there were still noises in the woods; now every sound was magnified. Strain as I might, I didn't see the red light again. We trotted as quickly as we could, Ed holding his shotgun and Ethel on her leash, and me holding the light, Old Dan, and Sambo. They kept trying to sniff at things, no doubt thinking we were looking for another coon. The moon had set, and the night seemed blacker than ever.

I could feel sweat dripping down my face and back. We finally found our way back to the tree line. That open field never looked so good!

Once the dogs were back in their kennels, Ed and I sat on his front porch, sipping ice cold Cokes. "Well, we know one thing," said Ed.

I nodded. "Yep, the red light story is real." I shook my head. "I don't want to do any more coon hunting, if it's all the same to you."

He looked at me. "Well, I do. But I don't intend to go into that thicket again. Dad must have seen it at some point, because he won't go in either. Of course, he tells me it's just because he doesn't want to fight through the thorns and bushes."

Suddenly I was thankful I had a protective mother, instead of an adventurous dad. "I guess there are some things that are just unexplainable."

A car pulled into the driveway. It was Ed's dad, back from his meeting. "Hi, boys," he said. "You're back sooner than I thought you would be. I even stopped over on Latham Road to see if I could catch you and maybe walk a ways with you. When I got out of the car, I heard the dogs barking, but sounded like they were pretty far off. "

We looked at each other. "Did you shut the car door?" Ed asked.

"Well, of course. I walked into the woods a little piece."

It was like someone let the air out of a balloon as I sank back onto the porch. We started laughing like hyenas, the relief was so great. That had been his car door we had heard! Then we proceeded to tell him about our scare. He laughed along with us, but then turned serious.

"What about the red light you saw? What do you think that was? I have seen it myself. I would guess it's some kind of reflection on some trash or something in there, maybe an old tail light on a junked car. "

Ed nodded. "It probably is."

"Say," said his dad. "wanta go see if we can find out what it is? This would be a perfect time. You'd never find it in the daytime. How about it, Champie? Son?"

I hung my head. I didn't care what it was. I wanted no part of it. But Ed jumped up. "Yes! That's a great idea! Then we can tell everyone we debunked the ghost story!"

Ed's dad slapped him on the back. "Let's go! Coming, Champie?"

"No, sir, if you don't mind. I'm pretty tired from all that walking. I'm not used to it."

He grinned. "Ok, you can stay here. We shouldn't be too long. Once we see it, we can just walk towards it until we get there."

They took off across the field. I laid down in the porch swing, which was cushioned, and soon fell asleep.

I woke up just before daylight with my arm asleep where I had lain on it. Everything was quiet except for the sound of crickets and a mocking bird that had started to sing. No sign of Ed or his dad.

I heard the screen door creak open. "Champie?" said Ed's mother as she stepped onto the porch. "What are you doing out here? Where's Mack and Ed?"

So I told her. They had not come back. She was sure they had met with an accident. They would not stay out all night on some wild goose chase, as she put it. "I'm calling the sheriff," she said, as she went back inside.

I wish I could say that everything turned out okay. But it didn't. After searching half the day, they finally found Ed and Mack, lying next to an old junk car in the thickest part of the woods. Both their throats were cut. Murdered in cold blood!

The scariest part was the autopsy showed that it wasn't a knife that did it. It looked like someone had ripped out their throats with long fingernails...or claws.

So no one ever goes into the woods along Latham Road. Searching for clues never turned up anything. Not even an old junked car. Years later, I still wonder what it is in those woods that waits for those foolish enough to go in.

DADDY'S GIRL

Doreen dusted the flour off her hands in irritation. Who could that be at the door? She hated to be interrupted when she was trying to make Daddy's favorite apple dumplings. Laying the rolling pin down, she wiped her hands on a wet dish cloth and took off her apron. Long skirts swishing, she hurried to the door.

She glanced into the parlor as she passed where Daddy sat in his wheelchair, by the window, just as she had placed him a few minutes ago. He dearly loved to sit and watch the birds and squirrels out the window. Poor dear, he had so little to entertain him these days.

Opening the large front door, she forced a smile as she greeted the two little old ladies on the porch. "Hello, Miz Chester, Miz Polk. How are you all today?"

The gray haired Mrs. Chester smiled back at Doreen. "We're just fine, dear. We just wanted to stop by and see how your poor daddy was doing."

"As well as could be expected, Miz Chester. As you know, he

suffered a debilitating stroke. He isn't able to receive visitors."

Mrs. Polk spoke up. "Well, we don't want to bother him, of course. Can you just tell him that we stopped by?"

"Of course," said Doreen. "He'll be cheered to hear it."

She waited until the two ladies were well down the long walk before closing the door firmly. Then she went into the parlor. "That was Miz Chester and Miz Polk, Daddy. They stopped to visit. I told them you didn't feel up to it."

Daddy just sat there, staring out the window. The stroke had left him unable to speak, but he and Doreen were so close, she could almost tell what he was thinking. She smoothed down his lap rug. "I'll just go and finish those apple dumplings for you! Then this afternoon we can have a nice cup of tea together." She smiled at him, tears starting in her eyes. She hated seeing him like this.

Doreen's father, John Fitzsimmons, had been a strong, influential figure in Dawson Springs. He had started a feed and seed business from scratch when he first came over from Ireland. It had been so successful that he had amassed a small fortune. He met Doreen's mother through her father, a local horse breeder and trader. He built this big house for her when they married.

The house stood on a huge bluff just outside the city and across from the Tradewater River. It was a handsome, two-story house with green shutters and a grand entrance. The front porch was surrounded by a decorative white rail which fanned out on either side of the front steps. Doreen's mother had loved her house and poured all her energy into it. She never had much time for Doreen after she found out that Doreen had rather read books than garden or arrange furniture.

Doreen's daddy's business kept him away from home quite a bit. She was an only child. She secretly thought that her parents never really wanted children. But since her daddy's illness, they had been closer than ever. Her mother had been dead for years and there was no one to take care of him but Doreen. He appreciated her now more than he ever had.

She soon had the dumplings made and cooling in the pantry. She checked on Daddy one more time; he sat as she had left him. He seemed to be enjoying the garden from the window. So she hurried to the cleaning closet and got a dust cloth. The furniture was beginning to need a good dusting.

They had had a cleaning lady come in twice a week until Mr. Fitzsimmons' stroke. Then Doreen had decided it was just too much commotion for him and decided to do it herself. It never occurred to her that she was taking on too much. Nothing was too good for Daddy.

It had been hard to keep people away. John Fitzsimmons was a popular man and of course, everyone knew him because of his business. But Doreen knew he would not want them to see him like this, and not being able to speak to them would be awful.

He could not move so much as a finger. Doreen had to bathe him tomorrow. He was starting to have an odor. She knew he would be furious if she didn't keep him clean. She wondered how she would do it. It was improper for her to see him naked; yet it had to be done. It worried her considerably.

When the doctor had come a week ago, Mr. Fitzsimmons had been in bed, barely breathing. He told Doreen he didn't expect him to last the night. Doreen had thanked him and let him out the front door and told him she would send someone to get him if she needed him.

She sat by Daddy's bed all night. He didn't seem to get any worse, so the next morning, she brightly told him, "Daddy, there is an old wheelchair that Mother used before she died. I'm going to get it and get you up out of that bed! You will get well a lot faster if you don't have to lie in bed all the time. Why, you might catch pneumonia!"

Somehow she managed to get him in the chair. He didn't weigh a lot, and Doreen was a strong girl. She knew she was doing the right thing. She could see the gratitude in Daddy's eyes. She kissed him on the cheek. "I'm going to take care of you from now on," she said gently. "You seem a little cold. I'll get a lap rug for you."

She went to the closet and took out her mother's buggy robe, which was never used now. Doreen was not one to go driving. She shook the dust out of it and put it across Daddy's thin legs.

"Now! You can come and look out the window while I fix our breakfast. Do you want an egg?"

Of course Daddy could not answer or even move a muscle. But she could see by his eyes that he was not really hungry. She sighed. She fixed two eggs and toast anyway and a pot of tea.

She tried getting Daddy to sip tea from a spoon, but he just was not able to swallow it; it dribbled down his chin onto his chest. Doreen dabbed at it with a napkin. "Daddy, you simply must take something." But he of course, did not answer.

She sighed. She ate her own egg and toast and quite enjoyed the Darjeeling tea they always special ordered from India.

"Daddy, I'm going to wheel you into the parlor. You always enjoyed sitting in there with your cigar. I'm sorry you can't have a cigar now." She looked at him expectantly, hoping the mention of one of his favorite pastimes would get some response.

When it did not, she wiped her mouth and his with a napkin and took him to the parlor window, where there was a flower bed with Hummingbird Vine. He would enjoy watching the little birds as he recuperated. She had no doubt he would recuperate, and dreamed of all the things they could do together, without Mother.

Maybe they could sail to the Continent. Or take a ride on a steamboat down the Mississippi. As the days passed, she began to suspect that Daddy was wheelchair bound for the rest of his life. His skin had turned gray and was beginning to sag. And there was the odor. She would have to give him a bath very soon. She shrank from the prospect.

So she didn't think about it. 'I don't have to do it today,' she thought. 'He'll soon be up and about, and can do it himself.' But she couldn't bring herself to do it that day.

So a few more days passed; it was a lovely summer. Sometimes after supper Doreen took Daddy out onto the veranda in the back. She told herself he would not want to sit on the huge front porch, where people could see him from the road. She could see him watching her as she darned some bed linens in the big rocking chair. It really bothered her that she couldn't do more for him.

The day she fixed the apple dumplings, he never ate a bite of them. So she enjoyed them herself, with some lemonade. She kept up a steady stream of conversation, about all the things that they would do once he was well. And best of all, Mother wouldn't be there to interfere. Mother had never wanted Doreen and her father to be close. She was jealous of Doreen and always shut her out as much as possible.

Of course, she didn't say these things to Daddy. He had loved her mother, and didn't notice the slights that were foisted upon Doreen. When she was a little girl, he used to swing her up in the air, her petticoats flying, when he would come home from work.

Mother always frowned, and said she would never be ladylike if he kept treating her like a tomboy. Daddy ignored her. Daddy was a man used to getting his way. Sometimes he would take her and Mother out in the buggy with him into the country, where they would enjoy a picnic under a green tree. Doreen wished it was just him and her. Mother always insisted she sit a certain way and make sure her skirt didn't ride up, and not to get jam on her blouse, and no, she could not go wading in the nearby stream. In other words, no fun could be had, as you had to be a lady at all times.

Doreen smiled. But now she had Daddy all to herself. This last year after her mother died, she was busy trying to keep the house and order the groceries, and she didn't have as much time to think about her relationship with Daddy. He was gone a lot because of his work.

Suddenly she listened in alarm. Someone was coming around the house! She jumped up, the linens in her lap tumbling to the floor, forgotten in her haste to protect Daddy from unwelcome visitors. He got tired so easily.

Hurrying down the veranda steps, she saw the doctor carrying his black bag. Her eyes widened. This would never do. Daddy wasn't up to an examination. Rest and quiet were what he needed!

"Doctor Brown! Why, what brings you here?" she asked, as she advanced on him.

He stopped. "I just thought I'd check on John while I was out this way. I see he's out in his wheelchair. That's great. The fresh air will do him good."

"Oh, yes, and he enjoys it very much. He told me just yesterday how much better he feels." She crossed her fingers. Of course, Daddy couldn't speak, but she knew he was enjoying being out.

The doctor craned his neck in the direction of the veranda. "I'll just step up and have a word with him. I must say, I'm surprised that he has rallied so well."

Doreen put her hand on his arm. "Well, he's asleep in his chair right now. He probably wouldn't want to be disturbed."

The doctor rubbed his chin. "Nonsense! He'll be glad to see me. Anyway, he's been cooped up for over a week. It'll do him good." And he walked around Doreen and started up the walk.

Doreen panicked. Daddy hated to be woken from a nap. What

was she going to do now? But the doctor was halfway up the steps and then striding across the porch. He knelt before the chair.

"John! John, old buddy, wake up!" Then his brow creased and he wrinkled his nose.

Doreen pressed her lips together. She knew she should have bathed Daddy, but it was just such an overwhelming prospect for a girl. And it would have been so difficult to get him out of the chair. She clasped her hands and wrung them.

"Doreen?" The doctor turned and looked at her. "How long has he been dead?"

Doreen burst into tears. "He's not dead, I told you he was napping! What a cruel thing to say!" And she buried her face in her hands.

She felt the doctor's gentle hands on her shoulders. "We'll have to get the undertaker."

She was filled with horror! No, they couldn't take Daddy away from her! She ran to the wheelchair and grabbed her Daddy by the cheeks. "Don't leave me, Daddy," she cried as the rotten flesh slid off in her hands.

Somehow the doctor got Doreen into his buggy and they went into town to get help. On the way, Doreen began to cry again. "Mother sent you, didn't she?" she sobbed. "She could never stand for me and Daddy to be together without her."

Doctor Brown was horrified. Doreen's mind had obviously turned and she was delirious. "Doreen," he said gently. "Your mother has been gone for more than a year."

"She's come back! She's come back and taken Daddy!" There was no consoling her.

When they got to the main road into town, the doctor turned and looked back at the house on the hill. It was then he saw a woman in the garden, in a long blue dress with a large hat and a basket on her arm. Mother had come back, after all.

THE MOONLIGHT CANOE TRIP

I was so excited about the canoe trip down the Tradewater! The moon would be full that night, and a large party of canoes would be setting off from Dawson Landing just off Highway 109 South.

My cousins, Diana and Vicki, would be riding with me in my canoe; well, technically it wasn't my canoe; I was renting it from the folks at the Landing. But it would be mine for the trip, and I was so looking forward to gliding silently down the stream under the moon.

"Are you ready to go?" asked Vicki as we arrived. "It will be so much fun!"

"I sure am," I replied. "Here, hold my camera and try to get some pictures while I'm paddling. Even though it's dark, the moonlight should make for some interesting contrasts in the woods."

Diana was carrying a small cooler. She held it up. "In case we get thirsty," she grinned. "Water and Cokes."

There were about 25 people there milling around when a voice came over the loudspeaker. "May I have your attention please? Everyone get your parties together, two or three to a canoe. Line up on the water steps and we'll bring the canoes over so you can get in. You may take off at any time after you are loaded in. And don't forget to put on your life jackets that are located underneath each seat!"

We joined the line, slowly moving toward the lighted steps that went down to the water. The managers held the canoes steady until everyone was in and had their life jackets on. We were the last ones, but it didn't take that long until it was our turn.

The night bugs buzzed around the large pole lights at the edge of the parking lot above. We could hear the river current and a few small splashes. The river looked black ahead. "Got your flash-lights?" asked the boat manager.

I pulled a medium sized flashlight from my small tote bag and held it up. Diana and Vicki showed him theirs as well, and soon he pushed us off, with Diana in the middle and Vicki and I paddling. We had both done this before, so we made good headway as we glided along downstream.

Soon we let the current carry us and just used the paddles to keep us in the middle. There were a lot of bends in the river, so the other canoes were soon lost to sight, even though we could hear voices and laughter ahead.

The moonlight through the trees dappled the black water. The night birds called in the deep woods bordering the banks. I sure hope we didn't get dunked. I imagined the water moccasins hiding in the depths. "Oh, get a grip," I thought.

"This is beautiful," said Vicki. "I'm so glad you had this idea!"

"Me, too," I said. "You okay there, Diana?" I asked, as I was sitting in the prow and she was behind me.

"Great!" she answered. "I'm just enjoying the ride, and not having to paddle."

We all laughed. As we slid along, our paddles splashing in the water, I thought about the Native American Indians, who used to travel the Tradewater regularly to the trading grounds in the big bend of the river.

I wondered if they ever traveled in the dark. It would have been difficult without flashlights. Then clouds covered the moon and I couldn't see much ahead. "Give me some light, Diana."

She clicked on her flashlight and shone it out ahead of the canoe. Good, we were still on course. About that time, I sensed, rather than saw, a presence beside our canoe, moving along with us. A creepy feeling swept over me.

Vicki sucked in her breath and stopped paddling. The stern of our canoe swept sideways. "Hey!" I said. "You better start paddling or we're gonna be…" but my voice trailed off, as I saw, running past me, a large canoe, very different than ours.

Something about it just made me feel strange. Maybe it was the managers of the canoe rental place, making sure everyone was all right. That had to be it.

"Hi," I tried to say, but my voice came out as a whisper. I watched as the large canoe swept on, paddled by at least six people, large men by the look of them. It was pretty dark, but I got an impression of glinting bracelets and long hair pulled back.

Vicki had put her paddle back in the water just as the moon was partially visible again. We were automatically paddling, but four or five more big canoes passed us on both sides like we were sitting still. In the moonlight, I saw the faces, painted Indian faces. The canoes appeared to be made of wood, not metal like the ones we had all taken from Dawson Landing. They were painted with all kinds of symbols that I couldn't quite make out.

We did not make so much as a squeak. We were too frightened. For their paddles made no sound and there was not even a breeze as they passed, even though they went so swiftly. They were bent to their task, fully concentrating on guiding their canoes. Some seemed to be grimacing as they pulled with long strokes.

The light came and went as clouds rolled across the face of the moon. I heard a whippoorwill somewhere off to my left. I was practically frozen in fear. I didn't dare look back at my cousins, for fear I'd run the canoe aground. It looked for all the world like a war party.

When the last canoe passed us and disappeared around the next bend, we all let out one collective sigh. "Tell me we did not just see that," said Diana.

"I wish I could," said Vicki.

I couldn't speak, my mouth was so dry, and goosebumps crawled all over my arms and legs.

"Water," I finally managed to croak. Diana fished out a bottle from her cooler and handed it to me after she had opened it. I managed to slip in a swallow or two without wrecking the canoe, and went back to paddling.

A cool breeze had sprung up, and the moon was starting to go down lower in the sky when we reached our destination, about five miles down the river. The landing there was more primitive than Dawson Landing, and we expected to find the rest of our party turning around, or resting on the bank.

There was no one there. We pulled over and beached our canoe and got out. "Whew! I'm tired!" said Vicki as Diana handed out more water.

We all looked at each other. "Where are the rest of the people that started out with us?" I said. "If they had turned around we would have met them. So did they go on up farther?"

"They must have," said Diana. She shrugged. "They will be late getting their canoes back, and the managers won't be pleased."

We sat and drank our water. It seemed like everyone was afraid to bring the subject mostly on our minds. I could still see those painted, grimacing faces. I shuddered.

Then I noticed the surroundings, as the moon had fully come back out. Even though the bank was low here, it was more grown up than it should have been. This was the turning around place for the canoes on the short trip downriver. The bank should have been trampled down and showing signs of many feet and markings where canoes had been pulled ashore. I noticed my creepy feeling had returned.

"Girls, something tells me this is not over yet." They looked at me, seemingly oblivious to what I was seeing.

Then Vicki said, "This doesn't look right. And where are the others? I don't like this."

Diana had a frightened look on her face. "Ssssh! Listen!" she said with a finger on her lips.

We all but stopped breathing, as a sound reached us, a steady regular beating. Indian drums! Impossible, yet there it was. Not too close, but not really far away either. I pictured the large canoes, the swiftness of their rowers. It had been a war party, for sure.

"Back in the canoe!" I said, with a sense of urgency. We must get back up the river without being seen. We started for the canoe, but then saw on the river, more large boats like the ones that had passed us. We turned and ran for the woods, not turning on our flashlights for fear of being seen.

When we had run about a mile, breaking limbs and crashing through bushes and thorns, we stopped in a thicket and peered back the way we had come. We didn't see or hear any signs of being followed. The sound of our breathing was loud in the darkness of the trees. "Well, if they were going to follow us, we made enough noise for a herd of elephants. I don't think they'd have any trouble," I said between pants.

My cousins were huffing and puffing. Although we were all in fairly good shape, the combination of the obstacles we had fought through and our fright made us feel all done in.

"This can't be happening," Diana whispered. "It just can't be happening. It's like we've gone back in time two hundred years!"

"Well, I'm not going back to the river. We need to find our way through the woods," said Vicki. I agreed, and soon we were tramping back the way we had come, listening for the sound of the water current so we didn't get lost, and moving a lot slower than we wanted to.

Diana had left the cooler back at the landing, and soon our thirst was maddening. Five miles in the dark, in the woods, albeit dappled by moonlight, was no easy hike. We were still afraid to turn on our flashlights except for brief periods to make sure we didn't fall down a bluff.

But we struggled on. It was dawn before we neared our departure spot. We could hear people in the woods, shouting and moving around. We began to shout back, and soon one of the canoe managers and a policeman came bounding toward us.

"Thank God!" said the manager. "Are you all all right? We've been looking for hours! When you didn't come back to the landing, we waited awhile, then sent a canoe down the river, and they saw no sign of you. But they found your canoe at the next landing."

"You wouldn't believe us if we told you," I said, warily. Because I knew that people who see ghosts are looked on as touched in the head.

The policeman took our statements, Vicki doing most of the talking, as she had always had a silver tongue and could charm the wings off a butterfly. "Sorry for causing all the trouble," she said. "We just wanted to explore the woods a little, and must have gotten lost. I'm surprised we found our way back at all."

"Well, all's well that ends well," said the policeman. He left in his patrol car.

"Did you get our canoe back?" I asked the manager.

"No, I left it there in case you found your way back to it. I thought maybe you might feel safe to go back to it after awhile."

My eyes widened. "Feel safe?" I asked.

He looked long and hard at me. "I think I know what happened." He put his hands on his hips, his tongue in his cheek, and nodded at me.

I stared at him. Finally, he said, "It only happens every once in awhile, not on any certain date. And not always on a full moon. I was hoping none of my customers would ever have to go through a fright like that."

"Yeah, those coyotes in the woods, they give a person the creeps," I tried.

Vicki and Diana looked at me incredulously. Vicki opened her mouth to speak, then thought better of it and turned away.

The manager snorted. "Coyotes. Right. Coyotes aren't that great at paddling…or drumming. Don't worry, I don't think you're crazy. I haven't told anyone, either. Your secret is safe with me."

My mouth dropped open. He had seen them, too! "What makes it happen?" I asked.

"Don't know. What I do know is that there was a huge, bloody war between the Iroqois and the Cherokee here in Kentucky. Legend has it that it was somewhere along the Tradewater. I think sometimes there are places where time overlaps another time. And that's why we see things from other times." He shrugged. "That's just my theory. But, everyone doesn't have these experiences. I think it takes a special kind of person. Some are sensitive to it and some are not.

The Tradewater seems to be one of those places. All along it, people tell strange tales and see strange things. But, as I said, not all people are aware. That's why I don't mention it. But I could see that you were lying to the cop. That's when I guessed what happened. And I'm sure he did, too."

My eyes widened. "Has he seen them, too?"

He nodded. "He and I saw them together when we were just teenagers, canoeing down the river on a night just like this one. It was scary, but kind of awesome, too."

We all smiled. "Yeah, it kind of was, wasn't it?" I said.

FAIRY HILL

It was high summer in 1959 when I came to live at Fairy Hill with my Aunt Martha, my father's sister. My father had gone to Europe on a business trip and my mother thought it would be a good idea for me to get some country air and some fresh garden food. I secretly suspected that she wanted the summer all to herself to entertain her friends and do what she wanted without the responsibility of a twelve year old.

"Why do you call this place Fairy Hill?" I asked Aunt Martha, looking around at the rolling hills surrounding her colorful cottage garden. I could see the tree line of the Tradewater River in the distance. It was truly beautiful, and if there were such things as fairies, I thought they would like it here.

Aunt Martha put down her knitting in her lap, and turned to face me. We were sitting in twin rockers on her front porch, which was filled with pots of red geraniums, yellow marigolds, purple heliotrope, and other plants I didn't know the names of. Some were in pots, and some hung from the rafters. Butterflies and bees buzzed happily around them.

"Well, now, that is for you to discover this summer for yourself, Allie. And I'm sure you will. But I'll tell you one thing, this is a happy place. There is no sadness and no frowns here. Even the air makes you want to sing and dance." She smiled at me. I smiled back. I did like this place.

The small house was situated on a hill overlooking the Tradewater River bottoms. The summer air was hazy in the distance, and the green trees faded to a soft gray-green the further off you looked. Aunt Martha had every kind of flower you could imagine, as well as a kitchen garden which yielded fresh vegetables, herbs, and even blueberries. There was an orchard with apple and pear trees. There was a well with the coldest, sweetest water I had ever tasted. A grape arbor in the back garden shaded an old wooden swing where I loved to take my sketch book and drawing pencils and try to capture the loveliness of the place.

We drove into town once a week in Aunt Martha's old blue Ford and got milk, fresh bread, and cheese from the farmer's market. We also picked up jars of honey and jam from some Amish people who were regular vendors there. Once in awhile Aunt Martha would buy a roast or a chicken from the butcher's shop. It wasn't long before I began to put on weight, which wasn't a bad thing, since I was skinny to begin with.

Aunt Martha was an excellent cook. I noticed that every night after dinner, she put out a small plate on the back porch steps with a few vegetables and a bite of meat if we had any that night. Then she would say, "Bless this food, bless the night, and may you be happy in your flight."

"What is that verse for, Aunt Martha?" I asked her one day. "Who is the food for?"

She smiled. "Why, for any traveler who might pass this way and be hungry. It is always good to share with others."

I didn't ask any more, but I wondered who might be passing Aunt Martha's back steps way out here in the country and would eat a plate of food that had been sitting out for hours. But I hated to ask too many questions. So I just nodded and went on.

At night I slept in a white iron bed in a room with white muslin curtains with little tassels around the edges of them. There were bookshelves that held my favorite Nancy Drew mysteries, as well as other novels for young people. My Friend Flicka was one I had read over and over. The full moon peeked in the window and the night breeze caressed me to sleep.

One morning I awoke to find it had rained in the night, and as I looked out the window toward the back garden, I saw a ring of white mushrooms that had popped up beside the path to the orchard. I pulled on my clothes and some sandals and ran outside.

As I bent down to look, I heard Aunt Martha say, "It's a fairy ring. They have been dancing in the rain."

I grinned at her. "Do they like the rain?"

"Oh, yes," she said. "They are like flowers. They love to soak up the rain."

I reached out to pick one of the mushrooms. "No, no! They

don't like their stools removed! " I looked up in surprise. Aunt Martha had sounded really distressed. Like she really believed in fairies!

"Sorry," I said sheepishly, still playing along.

"I'll tell you what, Allie," she said. "Would you like to make a fairy garden with a little house in it?"

"Oh, yes! That would be so much fun!" I said enthusiastically.

So after breakfast, we started gathering materials for our fairy house and garden.

Sticks, pieces of bark, interesting rocks, and acorn caps were some of the things Aunt Martha helped me collect. We chose a corner of the back garden under a large oak tree where she had planted hostas and ferns she had dug up from the woods. We chose some smaller plants as well, and soon had a little wood house built under one of the hostas with a bark and stick bench and an acorn bucket. We found moss and made a soft little bed inside the fairy house.

We sat back and looked at our handiwork. I could have sworn I heard a tinkling laugh somewhere. I shrugged it off as a bird in the nearby oak tree. Aunt Martha didn't appear to have heard it. "I think they will be pleased with this, "she said. "I haven't done this since I was a girl. I had forgotten how much fun it was."

"How will we know if they use it?" I asked her. "Maybe they'll leave a tiny thank you note. Or maybe if I come out here early enough I might catch one still asleep on the little moss bed."

"Oh, you'll know," she said, and winked at me mysteriously.

Why, she acted as if she really believed in them! This was such a fun game.

I smiled. It was a game, wasn't it? Oh, well, it was fun, and something to do. I determined that night that I would stay up late and sneak out and hide to see if the fairies came to the little house.

We brushed off our hands and clothes and went back to the house, where Aunt Martha scurried off to the kitchen to make a blueberry pie. I got my sketch book and pencils and went to the old swing.

I tapped my pencil against my chin. Now, if fairies were real, what would they look like? I had seen cartoonish pictures of them, of course. But somehow I didn't think our fairies looked exactly like that. I began to sketch a small face with rounded cheeks and drawn-down dark eyebrows. A short nose and a bowed mouthful of sharp teeth…where had that idea come from? I was looking down at a little malevolent looking creature that was nothing like the beautiful, ethereal fairies I had seen pictures of. His rather longish stringy hair hung around his shoulders. He had large ears the full length of his head.

It was almost as if he had just appeared on the paper without my having much to do with it. Suddenly I felt a little sharp pain on my leg. I looked down to see a little place no bigger than a thorn stick, but it was starting to bleed. Aunt Martha must have some gigantic mosquitoes out here!

I put down my pad and pencil and wiped the blood with a tissue from my pocket. It wasn't that bad, so I forgot about it when Aunt

Martha called me for lunch.

That night I went to bed as usual, after watching Aunt Martha put out the little plate of food. I now suspected it was for the fairies that might want a snack as they passed by. I had never thought to check to see if it was gone in the morning; though if it was, it may have been some feral cat or woods creature that ate it.

I kept myself awake until I heard her come upstairs and close her bedroom door. Then I crept out from under my covers, and went to the window. There was enough moonlight to make moving shadows in the old garden below. The silvery beams shone on the path and I could see fireflies flitting about in the night.

I had kept my clothes on, so it was easy to sneak down the stairs and out the back door, being careful to not turn the latch and lock myself out. Crickets sang in the dark and I could smell the fragrance of lilies and honeysuckle, along with the old fashioned roses. A slight breeze was blowing, and magic was in the air. I could feel it. Suddenly, in spite of my earlier doubt, I just knew fairies were about.

I made my way carefully across the garden, beneath tall sunflowers and hollyhocks. The fairy ring of mushrooms looked silver in the moonlight, and as I looked, the mushrooms began to sway. Excitement ran up my spine. I quickly sank back into the darker part of the garden, and kept my eye on the ring.

A wind chime tinkled somewhere nearby. Or was it a fairy laugh? I became aware of tiny flitting things whooshing past me and landing on the mushroom stools. It wasn't easy to make out just what they looked like; they were so small and moved so fast. I could faintly hear a tune that was hard to make out, but there just the same. It was as if the wind was humming a song I did not know. I was enthralled as the tiny beings slipped down off their mushroom stools and began dancing around in a circle.

I heard the wind chime sound multiplied now, as if dozens of tiny laughs drifted around the garden. I was enthralled. The fairies were actually real. I was still enough of a child to be thrilled at the sight, and to believe that I was not hallucinating.

I could not see them clearly, but got an impression of silky garments that floated in the breeze and double sets of wings, positioned sort of like a dragonfly's.

There was a crack of thunder then, and I felt a few droplets hit my arms. As the rain picked up, the fairies danced faster and faster and the night was filled with the sound of their tinkling laughter between claps of thunder. I hightailed it to the house, already soaked, but not wanting to get struck by lightning

About halfway up the path, I felt something on my shoulders and then a hurtful yank on my hair. I screamed and reached up, only to be bitten on the hand by what felt like sharp little teeth. I tried to knock whatever it was off. But it held onto my hair tightly.

I kept running, blinded now by rain and tears, and screaming at the top of my lungs. Of course, by the time I galloped up onto the back porch, Aunt Martha was there at the door. "Good heavens, child, get in here! You're soaking wet! Where have you been, and why?" She looked very worried and upset.

I grabbed her around the waist. It was a good thing she was wearing a thick robe or I would have soaked her pajamas. "Get it off! Get it off!" I cried hysterically.

She pried my arms from about her waist, and took my hand and led me to the bathroom, where she got a clean towel and started drying me off. "It's okay, it's okay, there's nothing on you. What was it?" She hugged me and tried to smooth my hair, which was tangled into mats.

"How on earth…" she began. I reached up to get the towel from her and she saw my hand, and gasped. "Your hand has been hurt! What happened?"

Haltingly, and through tears, I told her about wanting so badly to see if the fairies used the little house, and see them dance, and how I had hid in the garden and watched them. "Then, when it started to rain, I ran for the house, and one of them jumped on my back and started pulling my hair," I said. "I didn't mean any harm, Aunt Martha," I sobbed.

Aunt Martha looked more and more alarmed. "You actually saw them?" she asked. "Oh, my! But they would not harm you like that, even though it is forbidden for them to let mortals see them. I guess they didn't know you were watching. But someone did." She frowned.

She got up and began pacing back and forth. "It had to have been old Puck, the green man. He's the only one mean enough to do something like this. Not the fairies! I should have known."

"Green man?" I asked. I had heard stories of the Green Man, a nature spirit that lived in forests and woods.

"The green man has been around for centuries, though not many people believe in him anymore. But, here at Fairy Hill, he is very much in evidence. I have seen him myself. In fact, I have an old carving I picked up from a medieval church that was damaged in a fire and they decided not to rebuild. I'll get it." She went off to her bedroom.

I rubbed down the goosebumps on my arms. I was still upset, and these stories didn't help.

Soon Aunt Martha was back, with a small stone carving of a face I knew well. It was the very image of the little man I had drawn under the arbor in the swing. I was not really surprised. I must have turned pale, for Aunt Martha patted me on the back. "Allie? Are you all right?"

I nodded. Then I told her about the picture, and she asked me to get it from my room. When I brought it and laid it in her lap, she shook her head in disbelief. "I didn't even know what I was drawing," I confessed. "It was like, it just drew itself."

She nodded slowly. "He obviously is not pleased about something. I have noticed a presence in the garden in the trees, something that just seems to have slipped away right before I look. One time I thought I saw his face through the hedge. But why he would pick on you, I can't imagine. And I won't put up with it. Fairy Hill has always been a happy place, a joyful place, and I do my part to see that it remains so. And it shall!" she said firmly.

After brushing the tangles out of my hair, she accompanied me upstairs once again and tucked me into my bed. She closed the window firmly. "Don't be afraid, Allie. I will take care of this. I want you to be happy here, not scared."

Surprisingly, it didn't take me long to go back to sleep, and the next morning it all seemed like a dream. I could smell breakfast, so I hurried into my clothes and went downstairs to find Aunt Martha sipping her first cup of coffee. She smiled at me. "Sleep well?" she asked.

"Once I got to sleep, I did. Aunt Martha, how are we going to find out what the green man wants?"

"We are going to get out my old books about England. That's where he originated, you know. Then, when the English settled North America, he was brought along, evidently."

So after breakfast, we settled into her small library, which consisted of floor to ceiling shelves of books old and new, and a comfortable old fashioned pink chintz reading chair, all plump and stuffed, with a floor lamp on one side and a table on the other for whatever was needed.

Aunt Martha got out a stack of old literature and folklore books, which smelled of must and dust, but I loved the smell, because there was something mysterious about it, and also because I just loved books. We pored over stories about Puck and the green man, trying to find out what the people in ancient times believed about them.

"It says here that Puck sometimes would spin wool or shine shoes, and churn butter and other household chores, but if you angered him in some way, he would undo all he had done." She sighed and removed her glasses to scratch her nose. "I've never heard of the green man doing those things. In fact the more I read, the more I think they are two separate beings, even though I saw in one book that people sometimes used the names interchangeably."

I looked up from where I was stretched out on the floor with my own reading. "How could I have angered him, Aunt Martha? I didn't even know about him until I drew him. Maybe I'll put out some milk for him. That might help things a little. I read that people put things like that out for him sometimes."

She stuck her glasses back on. "That's it!" she exclaimed. "I have been putting out food for the fairies for years, and never a thing for Puck! He is probably getting tired of being ignored."

"I knew that food was for fairies! You said it was for travelers!"

"And so they are. For they fly and flit here and there, and go long distances in the night, or so I've heard," she said, her blue eyes twinkling.

"Heard where?" I asked suspiciously. I was beginning to think there was a lot more to Aunt Martha's fairy tales than she was telling.

"Well, since you have actually seen them..." She seemed to be trying to decide whether to tell me more. She snapped the book closed that was on her lap.

"One night I took a moonlight walk, down by the river. I was enjoying the summer air, listening to the night creatures, when suddenly I heard a faint moaning, kind of like a bird that was hurt.

I looked all around on the ground, because that is where it seemed to be coming from. Then I saw it. A tiny creature, all shimmering, with wings, only one was hanging at a crooked angle. I stooped down to see if I could help. I thought it was a big moth or something. Imagine my surprise when a little intelligent face looked up at me…a face that was almost, but not quite, human. I was quite shocked. My mouth must have dropped open. The tiny girl, for it was a female, plainly said "Help me! Please!" in a very faint voice. It is a wonder I could hear it from one so small.

"I whispered, not wanting to scare her. 'I will do what I can,' I said. I gently placed my hand on the ground and she climbed into it, being careful not to hurt her broken wing. I carried her to the potting shed, where I found some tweezers and sticks. I made her a little splint from sticks and twine to hold her wing in place, and then I gave her some water. It was very difficult. I had lit a lantern so I could see better, but she was so small, about the size of a dragonfly.

"That was my first encounter with the fairies at Fairy Hill. I hadn't named it that then. She told me there were others like her. She had broken her wing when being chased by an owl, and looking back, had flown into a branch. Her name was Rosamond.

"She stayed in my bedroom for a couple of weeks, while her wing healed. When she was able to fly again, she told the other fairies that I was a good person and would not try to harm them. Soon I was conversing with them in the woods and in the garden. I started leaving food out for them, and in the morning it's always gone."

"But what about Puck?" I asked.

Aunt Martha made a swatting gesture. "Him! Well, now, he is not a fairy, but a spirit of the forest. He has always been mischievous, but when he starts harming my niece…I have to find a way to appease him or run him off."

"We'll try a bowl of milk tonight." I said, not sure if that was enough. It didn't seem like something to bite someone over and mat up their hair.

Aunt Martha smiled. "That's a start," she said.

So that night we put out a big bowl of milk next to the plate of food for the fairies and Aunt Martha said her magic verse. "Bless this food, bless the night, may you be happy in your flight."

Puck was not amused. In the morning the milk had been turned over and spilled on the ground.

After breakfast, Aunt Martha took her gardening gloves, a hoe, and a basket, and started weeding the flower beds along the sides of the cottage. "I love this work," she said. "It's a big job to keep all these plants and bushes, but it is such a pleasure to grow things and see the beauty all around."

I was deadheading some marigolds as she talked. "It is pretty fun," I admitted. "But what are we going to do about Puck?"

"Let's just enjoy the day and not think about it for now. Something will come to us, I'm sure." Aunt Martha's worried look belied her cheerful words. We continued to work, loosening the earth, deadheading, and pulling weeds, which we dropped into the basket.

"Tomorrow, we'll fertilize everything," said Aunt Martha. She turned to me as she put the hoe away. "You're good help, Allie. I wish you could stay here all the time."

I smiled at her. "Me, too."I gave her a big hug. "Look, the sun is setting."

We had cold ham and cheese sandwiches and big glasses of milk for supper. For dessert, Aunt Martha pulled out an apple pie and cut us each a large wedge. It was the best supper I'd ever had.

We decided to sit on the front porch after supper in the old creaking swing, enjoying the fireflies among the flowers. Aunt Martha said her back was stiff, and she didn't know how much longer she could keep up the cottage gardens, along with the vegetable garden and the housework. "I'm getting on in years, you know," she said. And then, "Ouch!" She swatted the back of her neck.

"Mosquitoes?" I asked.

"Something bigger than that. Puck! You old rascal, show yourself!" But he did not, of course.

"He pinched me good," said Aunt Martha. "This has got to stop. Come on." And she got up and headed for the front gate.

We walked through the gate, across the road, and into the woods on the other side. It was dark by now, and there was a gibbous moon above, which helped light our way, but barely.

I noticed we were on a barely worn path that led into the woods. I could hear water ahead, and soon we came to the bank of the

Tradewater. An owl hooted somewhere, and I clutched Aunt Martha's hand. "Why are we here?" I whispered.

"We need help," Aunt Martha replied. "Sit down quietly and we will see if we get it."

We sat on the soft grass. "Now, just forget about everything and look around you. But try to look without thinking about what you actually see."

I was confused. How could I look without thinking about what I was seeing? "Huh?" I asked.

"Just relax," said Aunt Martha. She stared in one direction. "Just unfocus your eyes, sort of, like looking at one of those magic picture books."

I knew what she meant...the magic picture books that you could see what was there only if you looked at them in a certain way. "Oh. Okay," I said.

We sat there for a long time. I began to pick up on sounds I hadn't noticed before. Little rustlings, faint bird chirps, and snuffles of some small animal. I could smell the earth, the leaves, the water. My senses were on high alert. Soon I began to enjoy the night. It was then I heard something different.

Aunt Martha put her hand on my arm. "Sssh, do you hear that?"

I nodded. It was a soft sighing, singing kind of sound, like the wind through a chimney, only more musical. All of a sudden, the fairies came flitting along, tiny, ethereal creatures, shimmering like beams of light. One stopped, fluttering in front of Aunt Martha. "Rosamond," she said.

A very small musical voice answered. "It is I, Martha! Do you wish something?"

"We have a problem, dear Rosamond. Perhaps you can tell us what to do." And she told the story of how Puck had made himself known and was being a nuisance besides. "I don't know what he wants, or why he started doing this."

Rosamund put her small hand to her chin. Her beautiful little face pouted in thought. All the while her wings beat the air like a hummingbird's.

"I will talk to him if I can find him," she finally said. "unless he doesn't want to be found; but I will certainly try. This cannot go on! Fairy Hill is a happy place. It is one place that fairies feel most at home."

"Thank you, dear Rosamond!" said Aunt Martha. "I certainly hope you can talk to him. I will return here tomorrow night."

"Very well," said Rosamond, and flew off after the other fairies. Aunt Martha and I went out through the woods and back to the flower bedecked cottage, and after putting out the little plate of food, at last, we slept. Puck did not bother us any more that night.

I dreamed of fairies and flowers all night. They were good dreams, and I awoke feeling that things would be all right.

But when Aunt Martha and I went outside to fertilize the flowers, they had all been pulled up and trampled to shreds! All along the sides of the cottage, and in front of the fence, every bud and bloom was stomped into the ground. I started to cry.

Falling to her knees, Aunt Martha picked up some gladiolus, the roots still attached, shedding dirt on her dress. "That's the last straw!" she said. "Puck! Puck! Show yourself! I at least deserve to know why you are doing all this!"

She stood up, brushing her hands off. I would swear I heard a chortle of laughter, very briefly. I wiped my eyes and tried to stop crying. That wouldn't help matters.

"Nothing like this has ever happened at Fairy Hill," said Aunt Martha. "Who would want to ruin such a beautiful place? He must be really evil!"

I shivered. No telling what he might do next. I remembered the little sharp nip on my leg. Biting my lip, I followed Aunt Martha to the house.

That night, we went to the woods again and sat on the river bank. Rosamond came shortly after, flying around several times before settling on a rock near us.

"Rosamond! Do you have an answer for us?" whispered Aunt Martha.

"Yes, I do," the sprite answered. "Puck was hiding in a hollow tree not far from here, planning more mischief, no doubt. I demanded that he come out, or I would report him to the Elven king, who would send out his armed forces and pull him out. That got his attention!" She folded her small arms across her chest.

My eyes were wide. An Elven king! It sounded more and more like a fairy tale. 'Wait,' I thought. 'It is a fairy tale!' Trying not to giggle, I strained to hear what Rosamond had to tell us. This was really not a laughing matter.

"As you know, Puck is the spirit of the forest. He takes care of the trees, the streams, the flowers, everything. It is his job. Oh, he likes to play tricks now and then, but I have never known him to be mean and hateful before. So I just asked him why he is doing these things to you and Allie."

He told me that he resents that you have taken over his job. When you moved to Fairy Hill, you started planting and weeding, dividing, and fertilizing, and he didn't have anything to do there. He had taken care of all of it before. This is an old forest; it mostly takes care of itself. So Puck wanted to drive you out, or at least, stop you from gardening. He knew you would do anything to protect Allie; that is why he picked on her to get your attention. And that's it." Rosamond spread her tiny hands.

Aunt Martha's mouth was open. "Why…why…I had no idea! My uncle left me the place when he died. I had not seen him in years. I just fell in love with it when I saw it. I always assumed he was the gardener! I was determined to keep Fairy Hill looking beautiful. Of course, it wasn't called Fairy Hill then. But after I discovered there were real fairies around here, the name seemed perfect. And I do so enjoy gardening! I wasn't trying to take it away from anyone!"

Rosamond smiled. She circled around Aunt Martha and waved her hands. "I have an idea!" she chimed.

"If you will give Puck back most of the garden, I think he would be satisfied to let you tend the vegetables, and the potted plants. Would that do?"

Aunt Martha nodded. "That would be good. I was just telling Allie that I was slowing down and didn't know how long I could keep up the place."

About that time, several other fairies flitted up near us. They seemed to glow with an otherworldly shine. Some were green, some pink, and some blue. They were the most beautiful things I had ever seen.

"Ahemmm!" I heard someone clear their throat behind us. We turned and there was a little man about three feet tall, wearing a brownish coat, pants, and a pointed hat. His face was the face I had drawn on my pad! It was the elusive Puck, turning up at last!

He took off his hat and bowed to us. "That will be a fine arrangement," he said in a voice that reminded me of the croaking of a bullfrog. Then he snapped his long, bony fingers, and was gone.

"How can I ever thank you, dear Rosamond?" said Aunt Martha.

"With some more of your delicious human food," twinkled Rosamond. She and Aunt Martha grinned at each other. Then she was off through the woods, the other fairies trailing along behind.

We made our way back to the house, and when we got up the next morning, lo and behold, all the flowers were back in the ground, looking as bright and fresh as ever! In fact, they looked more beautiful than they were before.

We had our breakfast on the porch just so we could admire them. Fairy Hill was once more a happy place! And Aunt Martha was able to do just enough gardening to keep her occupied and happy.

She has passed on now, leaving Fairy Hill to me. I know better than to do anything in the flower gardens. But my fruits and vegetables are most abundant and tasty. And I wouldn't be surprised if I didn't have a little help with those also.

OLD NETTLES' STORY

It was a warm summer evening with a bright full moon hanging over the silvery fields and lighting up old Ben Nettles' front porch. The stars hung like sparkling lanterns in the sky, and in the country along the Tradewater River, it seemed as if you could reach out and touch them. I breathed in the scent of pines and new-mown hay, along with a subtle fragrance I couldn't define, reminding me of honeysuckle. But it was already August and I knew the honeysuckle blooms were long gone.

I was one of three young men from nearby Dawson Springs who had come to stay at the farm for a couple of weeks, helping Old Nettles, as we called him, gather in his hay crop and store it in his barns for the coming winter.

Old Nettles was well-known around the area as a story teller, and this particular night he was entertaining us with a story that he swore was true. If it was, I was glad the place he talked about was gone, and the people with it. I was lounging on the old rug laid on the swing, slowly creaking back and forth, while my friends Nick and Jim were sitting on the porch boards with their backs against the wall, smoking. I didn't smoke myself, having decided it was a nasty and expensive habit. Old Nettles sat in his rocker, which looked like it had been around since Methuselah was a pup, puffing on his old pipe.

"Well, here's what I know about Woodson's Store," he said, as he tamped down his tobacco and relit his pipe, which had gone out. "I was just a little lad when my pappy and mammy bought this house and farm here. Now about a half mile over thataway," he said, gesturing to the north, directly in front of the house, "was an old store. It was a general store, meanin' they had all kinds o' stuff, from pots and pans, chewing tobaccer, tools, to bib overalls. You could get most anything there, candy, beans, dress material, lanterns, harness…well, you see what I mean.

"Anyways, Pappy never liked to go there much, and would usually hitch up old Betsy, our plow horse, who doubled as a buggy and wagon horse, bein' as we didn't have enough money to have a separate horse for the buggy and the wagon, and he'd drive plumb into town for most of our supplies. I didn't know why at that time, cause I was fascinated by all the goods the Woodsons had for sale, especially the hard candy.

"When we went there out of necessity, such as when Pappy didn't have time to go into town and needed somethin', I noticed that he just bought what he needed and never looked Woodson or his wife in the eye, and got out of there. Bein' a kid, I didn't think too much about it, but I used to think about that candy a lot. Candy was a special treat to me, you see, not like today, when kids have it all the time.

"There were rumors that started goin' around about these Woodsons. Pappy had heard 'em in town, I reckon. The rumors was that when a drummer (or salesman; they called them drummers then) of some kind of goods would go there to sell them stock for their store, the Woodsons would feed him a good dinner, be real nice to him, and invite him to spend the night in their spare room over the store. They lived in a little cabin right behind the store. Sometime in the night, old Woodson would creep up into the room where the drummer was asleep, get him to come downstairs on some pretext, and kill him with an axe and take all his money. Then his wife would help him raise up a patch o' floorboards behind the counter in the store and they would dig a hole and bury him, first chopping him into pieces, so he'd fit easy, y'know."

Here Old Nettles stopped and relit his pipe. The hair on the back of my neck was standing up. I thought he was just trying to entertain and scare us a little, but something about the way he told it, it had the ring of truth.

"Geez," said Jim softly. I noticed everyone's eyes were glued on Old Nettles, as he shifted and got more comfortable in his rocking chair.

"Well, as I was sayin'," Old Nettles went on, "people said that when the drummers weren't heard from, the company would send someone down to check on them."

"Why did they call them drummers?" I asked. I don't know

why, because it sure wasn't the main part of the story. I was just curious, I guess.

"Because they was drummin' up business, you might say. But, gettin' back to the story…when these company men would come, the Woodsons would be as nice as you please, and tell them yes, their man had been there and had sold them some extremely fine goods. They would feed them, be nice to them, and send them on their way. I assume the company men thought their drummers were highly unreliable people who had sold the goods and absconded with the money. And there old Woodson would be smiling and sharpening his axe for its next grisly job.'

I shuddered. "But what about their vehicle? I mean, they must have come in a vehicle of some kind."

"Now, Bill, remember, this was horse and buggy days. It woulda been easy to just chop up a drummer's wagon with that axe, turn it into firewood, and either put the horse in with theirs, or take it somewhere a good distance away, and sell it. No one knows for sure."

"Anyway, it's just a story, right?" I asked hopefully, not believing, but enjoying the slight chill I felt.

Nick and Jim chimed in. "Yeah, a good story, but not true, huh?"

At this Old Nettles looked at all of us, and drew on his pipe. Around the smoke his eyes narrowed. "But it is true, every word," he said.

"How do you know?" asked Nick.

"Because," Old Nettles said, "I was there."

After we all gasped, you could hear a pin drop. A mosquito lit on my arm and I jumped like it was the edge of old Woodson's axe. I slapped it, and letting out my breath, whispered, "Tell us."

"Well, as I already said, I thought about that candy at Woodson's Store. I thought about it a lot. I was about 8 years old at the time. Pappy would give me a nickel once in awhile, and not going anywhere much and not having anything to spend it on, I had quite a few nickels saved. I kept them tied up in a handkerchief underneath my mattress.

"Well, one night, the moon was full, just like it is tonight. I decided I would go to Woodson's and get me some of that hard candy I liked so well. Being just a little feller, I didn't realize you should go to the store in the daytime, and anyhow, it was still pretty early, probably about 9:00. I figured Mr. Woodson would still be up. So I started out across the field right there, and I was very excited. The moon had just risen and lit up the field so's I didn't need any kind of a light. It wasn't far, as I said before, about half a miile.

"Soon I could see light gleaming through the trees. I could just taste that sweet lemon and strawberry candy. When I came up to the edge of the woods right at the clearing where the store was, I could see a large wagon pulled up to the porch. The horse had been unhitched and I could see it tied to the rail. I started to cross over to the front porch of the store. I could see a light inside, so I knew they were in there. I saw someone cross in front of the window.

They had something held high over their head. It was such a quick movement that I didn't see who it was.

"Then I heard a thunk-thunk sound. Someone cried out, and then a thud! My eyes musta been like saucers. I could not imagine what it was, but had the feeling it was something bad. I should have turned around and run home right then, but curiosity and a kind of dread drew me toward that window. I scooted across the clearing as fast as I could. The night was very warm, like tonight. I could hear crickets in the grass and an old hoot owl off in the woods to my right. These sounds seemed magnified, as if they were trying to warn me not to go up there. But I ducked down underneath the window and slowly raised up to where I could barely peek inside."

By now we were all sitting up straight, straining to hear the next part of the story.

"Boys," said Old Nettles, "I got to see a man about a dog." And he got up and headed into the house to the bathroom.

All our collective breaths whooshed out as one. "Golleee!" exclaimed Nick.

"Of all times," said Jim.

I didn't say anything. I was caught up in the horror of the thing. I got up and paced until Old Nettles came back and sat back down in his chair. "Do you think it's getting late enough to go to bed?" he asked, and I could almost see his eyes twinkling.

"Awww, noooo!" we chorused as one.

"All right, then." He crossed his hands over his overalls and continued. "Well, I don't know what I expected, but it was even worse than I thought. I could make out something lying on the floor in front of the counter. Then I saw the axe come down. Thunk, thunk, thunk thunk! And then I saw the blood. Something moved behind the counter, and my attention was drawn to Mrs. Woodson, who had just moved back there. She bent over where I couldn't see, and I heard Mr. Woodson say, "Get the trap door open. Is my shovel handy?"

"She mumbled an answer and he stooped down and picked up an arm in a coat sleeve that was dripping blood. Well, I didn't hang around after that. I was back across that field as fast as my little feet could carry me. My heart was pounding out of my chest. I didn't notice the drummer's horse (for that's whose it was) had broken loose, sensing something was not going right with his master, and maybe scenting the blood, and had taken off galloping in the same direction I was going. I heard the hoofbeats behind me and imagined that it was old Satan himself, or maybe Mr. Woodson, who had grown hooves and was chasing me down so I couldn't tell what I had seen. Yessirree, it's a wonder I didn't have a heart attack. But I made it home, finally looked behind me in time to see the horse wheel to the left and go down the road like the demons of hell were after him, and perhaps they were.

"I pounded on the front door screaming for my pappy, and by the time he got there and opened the door I was crying so hard I couldn't talk. After awhile, I told him what I had seen and his face turned as white as the face of that moon is right now. I thought he was going to faint. He grabbed me to his chest and held me so tight that it was troublesome to breathe.

'I knew something was not right about those people,' he said. Then he called for Mammy to bring a lamp and get him his shotgun. He saddled up and rode to town and got the sheriff out of bed. By the time they got out to Woodson's, they pretended to be asleep.(Pappy told me all this later.)

The sheriff demanded that they open up and when they wouldn't answer, he broke the lock on the door and he and Pappy went in. Pappy said you could smell the blood and even though the floor had been scrubbed, it was still damp in front of the counter. The sheriff went behind the counter and pulled the rug back, and there was the trap door. He didn't open it then, but he and Pappy held the Woodsons at gunpoint and made them get on their horses with their hands tied behind their backs, and leading their horses, took them in to jail.

"Now, Pappy said that when that trapdoor was opened, there was a deep crawlspace down there and the earth had been turned up in several places. They dug up the remains of four drummers that their bosses thought had run off with their money, but instead had met their horrible fate at the hands of the Woodsons."

We all breathed a sigh of relief. It was surreal, sitting on the peaceful front porch on this fragrant summer night, knowing what had happened just across the field. "What happened to the old store?" I asked after awhile.

"Oh, there ain't nothin' there now," said Old Nettles, waving his hand. "They tore it down not long after the trial, the cabin, too. The Woodsons were hung. They don't hang people nowadays, but back then, that's how it was. And they got less than they deserved, at that. I still have nightmares about it."

I shook my head. "I'll bet." I looked across the field in the direction where it had all taken place. It seemed to me, as I sat there, that I could just see a faint glimmer of light between the trees.

MAGNOLIA BLUFF

"Mommy! Mommy!" screamed my four year old son as he rocketed into my bedroom, slamming the door. I woke up and held him as he shivered against me.

"What's wrong, Sandy?" I asked gently as he continued to sob. "It's okay, Mommy's got you. Was it a bad dream?"

He shook his head. "No, it was real! It was real!"

I stroked his back and tried to calm him. "Tell me about it."

"It was a ghost, and it tried to get me! I'm not going back in that room, ever!"

I sighed. People had told us this house was haunted right after we moved in. And Sandy had been listening to the stories, even though I didn't realize it at the time. And now he was seeing things that weren't there and hearing things in the night.

"All right, what did this ghost look like?" I asked. I hoped to show him it was something normal in his room.

It—it was all white and floaty, like this…" He waved his arms up and down slowly.

"Okay. Lie down beside me and go to sleep. I'll be right here."

He relaxed beside me and soon was back to sleep. It was a long time before I could sleep. My husband was out of town on business, leaving me to get unpacked from the moving and take care of Sandy.

We had come through Dawson Springs on a vacation from our home in northern Indiana. We had fallen in love with the small town, its hiking trails, nearby state park, and of course the Tradewater River, where we went on a canoe ride.

When we found out this lovely house and 3 acres was for sale on top of the bluffs overlooking the river, we jumped at it. It was a very reasonable price, and we were looking to get away from the city, and raise our son in a safer and healthier environment.

The house was a large frame house built in the craftsman style, with a nice front porch with thick posts of river rock and and a board and batten ceiling. There were two gigantic magnolia trees in the front yard. It was a two-story, with a big living room with a fireplace at one end (strictly decorative, the real estate agent told us), and a dining room, two bedrooms, a large bathroom, and a sunroom at the back. The kitchen had recently been redone with granite countertops and white painted cabinets. I loved the house when I first laid eyes on it. Upstairs were two more bedrooms, one with a full bathroom, the other with a half.

My husband Greg was also impressed. And when we walked outside at the back, the view was breathtaking. There was a nice wooden fence at the back of the yard almost on the edge of the high bluff. You could see the river below and also the rolling forested hills out beyond.

Sandy was running around and around in the back yard pretending to be a puppy. "Yip yip! I like this yard! Yip! Yip!"

Greg turned to him and said, "You know, you could actually have a real puppy here."

The grin on Sandy's face made up our minds. We could buy the place and put our home in Indiana up for sale. I turned excitedly to Greg. "We'll call it Magnolia Bluff, "I said, thinking about the two big magnolias in front. He smiled and agreed.

Greg had to take off almost as soon as we moved. He is a salesman for a mine equipment company, so I was used to his traveling quite a bit.

I went into town for some groceries and also stopped by the city offices to get some information about things to do, etc. I met several interesting people. The grocery clerk, whose name tag said "Jen", asked me if I was the person who had bought the house on the bluff. I told her I was, and she launched into a story about how people said the house was haunted.

I was kind of surprised. "I don't believe in ghosts, myself," I said, smiling at her.

"Well, no one has ever been able to stay there for long. Good luck," she answered, with a worried look.

We'd been there almost a week and I'd almost forgotten about the ghost story until the night of Sandy's nightmare. Because I was determined it was just a nightmare. I didn't argue with my son, though. I wanted to show him there was nothing to be afraid of.

The next morning when we went down to breakfast, I couldn't find my skillet I usually fried eggs in. "Sandy, honey, have you seen my skillet?" I asked, turning to where he was playing with a small car at the table.

"Nope," he said, not taking his eyes off of the car. I began to look all around the kitchen. It was the first room I had unpacked, because I knew I would need it the most. All my other pots and pans were in the cabinets where I had placed them.

I stood up and looked very carefully around the kitchen. There it was, under the table! I grabbed the non-stick skillet . "Now, how did it get down there?" I asked, immediately suspecting Sandy.

When I looked at it, I gasped. There, scratched deeply into the non-stick coating, was a message. "Go away!" I almost dropped the skillet. I knew Sandy didn't do this. I set it on the stove.

I turned to Sandy. "How about some cereal instead of eggs this morning?"

"Okay, Mommy, the ones with the dinosaurs!"

When he was happily downing the cereal, I started the coffeepot and then made myself two pieces of toast with butter and strawberry jam.

I was very uneasy. Who would want to do such a thing? And how did they get in? I had double locked all the doors before going to bed. It was a habit, since Greg was gone so much. If someone thought they would scare us away, they had another think coming.

I told Sandy I was going out to the newspaper box and would be right back. Then I thought, if someone had gotten in, they could come back in, and until I knew how it had happened, I didn't need to leave Sandy alone. "Why don't you go with me?" He readily agreed.

We strolled down the driveway to the road where the mailbox and paper box were side by side. It was a lovely morning, early summer, and the magnolia trees were in full bloom. I looked around to see if I saw anything out of the ordinary, but it all looked peaceful and nothing was out of place. I looked for footprints, but the grassy lawn and gravel drive would not show anything. .

That night, after Sandy had gone to bed, I called Greg on his cell and told him what had happened. He was upset and told me to get the locks changed the very next day. I assured him I would.

Sandy came and got into my bed at bedtime and I refrained from commenting. If someone was getting into our house, I wanted him right there. I made sure my bedroom door was locked before we went to sleep.

It rained in the night, and we slept kind of late. The clock said 8:30 when I sat up and rubbed the sleep out of my eyes. Sandy stirred beside me. He had had no nightmares that night.

When we went out on the porch to go and get the newspaper, I saw large, muddy footprints all over. I froze. It looked like a man's galoshes. They came up to the front door, and then went across the porch to both ends, with little scuffs around the windows, like someone was looking for a way in.

Sandy didn't appear to notice, so we continued to the paper box. When we got back, I settled him at the table with some crayons and a coloring book. I looked up the sheriff's number, took the phone off the hook, and went around the corner into the dining room where he wouldn't hear.

"This is Sarah Crandall. We just moved into the house up on 672 that overlooks the river?"

The sheriff said, "Why, yes, Mrs. Crandall. I know the house. What can I do for you?"

So I told him about the footprints on the porch, but didn't tell him about what Sandy had thought he'd seen. "And a few nights ago, someone must have gotten in the house, because one of my skillets was all scratched up. I mean, there was a message in it."

"A message?" asked the sheriff. "What did it say?"

"It said, 'Go away.' There must be another way into the house that I don't' know about, because everything was locked up. Do you think you could send someone out to look around?"

"Sure, I'll come myself. And, Mrs. Crandall, I'd suggest that you change your door locks. Just in case."

"I was going to do that. Do you know of a reliable locksmith I can call?"

"Yes, in fact, I'll call Bayer's Hardware myself and have them send a guy out that I know is trustworthy. Give me about half an hour."

"Thank you so much, Sheriff," I said as I hung up.

When I turned around, I jumped when I saw Sandy standing right behind me. How much had he heard?

"Mommy, come look at my lion I colored!" he said, smiling.

"Sure, Honey!" I was relieved he had not overheard my conversation.

Then I began to wonder what he had actually seen in his bedroom. 'Stop it,' I chided myself. 'It was just a bad dream.'

The sheriff, Mack Thornton, came and introduced himself, then took a pretty thorough look around the house, and checked the basement, which had locks on all the windows. They were shut tight and none of the locks had been tampered with. "I can't see any effort anywhere to get in," he said. "If someone does have a key, they won't be able to come in again once the locks have been changed. Bill Bayer should be over soon to do that. That message on the skillet was a pretty nasty trick. I don't know why someone would want to do that to you. But if you need anything at all, Mrs. Crandall, call me."

"I will, Sheriff, thank you." I watched his cruiser go down the drive and turn back towards town.

Bill Bayer from the hardware store soon arrived, and had all the locks changed in a short time. "That ought to do it," he said. I got out my checkbook and waited for him to figure up the bill. As Sandy was out of earshot, I decided to find out more about the house if I could.

"I want to ask you something," I said.

"Sure." He looked up at me. "Anything."

"Are you familiar with this house at all?"

He looked quizzically at me. "Well, yeah, I guess you could say that. I mean, I have never been inside or anything, but it's been here longer than I have."

"Have you ever heard any stories about it?"

"Oh, you mean the ghost stories? Oh, yeah, most of the people in town have. But I don't believe that stuff."

"I don't either. But…"

"But what?" He placed his hands on his hips and waited.

"Oh, nothing. I was just curious. That's all." I decided the less said the better. I didn't want it to get around town that the new lady was seeing things already.

He smiled, took my check, and turned to go to his truck. "Well, good luck, and hope all goes well." He gave a wave and was gone.

I pressed my lips together. A common ordinary prowler, that's all it was. Coupled with Sandy's dream, it seemed scarier than it had to be.

I busied myself the rest of that day scrubbing and cleaning the kitchen and putting the rest of the household items away that had still been packed in boxes. I felt very safe now that the locks were changed, and when we went to bed, Sandy settled in his room without protest, having apparently forgotten his fright from the night before.

But around midnight, I heard a great crash downstairs. I sat straight up in the bed. It sounded for all the world like a gunshot! My heart was pounding as I got up and reached for my robe on the bedside chair. Shrugging into it, and slipping my feet in to my house slippers, I hurried to the door and leaned my head out and listened.

Sandy didn't make a sound, so I crept to his room and looked in. He lay in fetal position, fast asleep. So he hadn't heard it at all. Strange…

I could hear the hall clock ticking in the silence that followed. I strained my ears as hard as I could. Slowly, I went down the stairs, listening at every step. There was a night light in the hall by the stairway. I couldn't see anything moving down there. I knew no one could get in, but was worried about what the noise was. It must have been outside.

Maybe some hunters, I thought. All of a sudden, I heard it again! I grabbed the front of my robe and opened my eyes wide. It sounded like it was right outside of the front door! That was it. I raced to the phone on the kitchen wall and frantically dialed 911.

"Someone is shooting a gun on my front porch!" I shouted. "Get the sheriff out to 1300 Highway 672! I am here alone with my four year old son. Hurry!"

The operator assured me help was on the way. I flew back upstairs to Sandy's room. He was still asleep. I couldn't believe it.

I looked out his window, which was above the front yard, and finally saw the blue lights coming up the drive. Hurrying down to open the door, I almost fell into Sheriff Thornton's arms. I was so shaken I could hardly talk.

I finally was able to tell him all about the incident over a hot cup of tea in my kitchen. It did little to warm me. I was covered in goosebumps and shivering. The sheriff got an afghan off the couch in the living room and wrapped it around my shoulders. "And your son slept through it?" Kids are amazing." He shook his head.

His deputy was with him, and was looking around the house outside. He was soon back to report that he had found no footprints or any other sign that anyone had been there. Nothing around the house appeared to have been disturbed. "I even walked out around the perimeter to see if I could find and shotgun casings, but there was nothing."

"Thanks, Ted," said Sheriff Thornton.

"Sheriff? The other families that have lived here…what kind of phenomena did they report seeing and hearing?" I was not sure I really wanted to hear his answer.

He scratched his head and looked down. "Well, mainly just noises and stuff. Nothing this loud, though. I always put it down to old houses creaking in the night, you know."

"Has anyone ever seen anything?" I told him about what Sandy said about the ghost in his room.

He sat up straighter in his chair. "Actually, they have. That is, no grownups have. But kids have. I figure it's the power of suggestion, you know, kids hear things from other kids. Then first thing you know, someone thinks they see a ghost."

"Well, Sandy knew nothing about the ghost, but he thinks he saw one the other night. He insists he was not dreaming. I want to get to the bottom of this. Who built the house? Do you know?"

"Well, it was a little before my time. Rumor has it that it was this old man named Jeremiah Stone. He was a recluse type, wanted solitude, and all that. This place has that, and yet is not too far from town. No one seemed to know much about him, because he didn't socialize."Sheriff Thornton stopped, and seemed to catch himself.

"In fact...." He stopped, rubbed his chin, and looked at me.

"What?" I was warmed up now, and had calmed down at last. "Does he have relatives, or anyone who would want to scare someone off the property?"

"He never had any family that I know of. At least they weren't around here."

The deputy spoke up. "Didn't he used to run people off with a shotgun? "

Sheriff Thornton and I both turned to stare at him. He turned red. "Maybe I shouldn't have said that. But that is what I've heard." He looked down at the floor.

"Well, he's been dead for forty years, so I doubt if it was him tonight," said the sheriff. "Probably a bunch of kids just trying to get a rise out of Mrs. Crandall." He turned back to me.

"Don't you worry, Mrs. Crandall, I will make regular patrols by here from now on. When is your husband coming home?"

"He should be in on Friday afternoon. He'll be home all week-end, and maybe even Monday. This is Wednesday, so surely I can make it until then. I don't believe in ghosts, and if I know you are passing by frequently, it'll make me sleep better. Now that the locks are changed, I know no one can come in." I stood up, and so did the sheriff.

"Well, I'm glad you got that done. We will sure keep an eye

out. Good night, Mrs. Crandall."

"Good night, and thank you," I answered, as I accompanied them to the front door.

When they drove off, I locked the door securely and went upstairs to look in on Sandy. He had rolled onto his back, and was lightly snoring. I kissed his forehead, tucked his blanket in, and made my way back to my own bedroom. I slept undisturbed the rest of the night, of which little was left.

Breakfast on Thursday morning was cheerful, Sandy eating the scrambled eggs I made in another skillet I pulled out. I had not thrown the scratched one away. I wanted Greg to see it. I sat on the front porch later and watched Sandy racing around the yard, pretending to be an airplane, then a choo choo train, and finally, when he wore himself out, we went in and settled in the wing chair in the living room for a story.

He chose a Winnie the Pooh book, and he was asleep before I reached the last page. I eased out from under him, laid him on the sofa and covered him with the afghan.

I had been wanting to experiment with a new cookie recipe I had found in a magazine, so I went out to the kitchen and got out the baking supplies. When I had them in the oven, I checked on Sandy, saw that he was still asleep, and went back to wash the utensils and bowls I had used.

I found myself thinking about the old man, Mr. Stone, who had built the house. It was a wonderful house, not something you would expect an old crabby recluse to put so much work into.

By the time Sandy woke up to the smell of the freshly baked cookies, I had decided I'd go into town to the newspaper office and library to see what I could find out about the house and the man who had lived there.

Sandy had what I thought was another bad dream that night. Once again, he woke me with his cries. But when I ran to his room, I was horrified. The rocking chair in the corner was rocking furiously and there was an atmosphere in the room that I could only describe as angry and disturbed. I grabbed Sandy from his bed and held him tightly. "What do you want!" I shouted. "Get out of here!"

I didn't wait for the answer, but ran back to my room with my boy in my arms and locked the door and shoved a chair under the doorknob. So much for new locks.

After soothing the crying Sandy back to sleep, I sat on the side of the bed. I was beginning to realize that this was no ordinary human mischief. I needed help. I shook my head. I'd never have thought that I would be considering the possibility of a ghost.

I sat up the rest of the night and nothing else happened. Sandy woke up early, rubbing sleep from his eyes. "Mommy!" he cried and hugged me tightly. "I saw the white thing again! But you came and got me."

"Of course, I did, Honey," I said softly. "Nothing is going to hurt my Sandy. It's not anything that can hurt you, and we are going to get rid of it. Until then, how would you like to sleep in here with me?"

He smiled. "Oh, yes, I would like that!"

I didn't know how Greg would take that, but he'd just have to live with it. I didn't expect him to put up much of a fuss.

Sandy and I went into town right after breakfast to the library. The librarian, Mrs. Bunch, was only too happy to give us library cards and show Sandy the children's section. While he looked at picture books, I asked her if she knew anything about our house and had any history there about it. She assured me that she did have an older yearbook from the Hopkins County Historical Society with a story about the house.

She got it for me, and I read about how it was a classic example of the craftsman style and had been built around 1900. Craftsman style homes had originated in the mid-1800's in England. With their sturdy brick or stone porch pillars topped by tapered posts, they were most often simple in design. Most were one story, but some had two stories, like ours.

Mr. Stone must have been quite proud of his home at one time, to have put so much work into it. The article said he had built a lot of it himself, with the help of local builders. He had come to Dawson Springs from New York state, a widower with no children. He must have been friendlier in life than he was in death, because the author of the article had talked with him at length.

"Mr. Stone built this house in memory of his late wife, Regina, as a tribute to her that she would have been proud of had she lived. She was killed in a horse and carriage accident not long after they were married. He never remarried, and had desired to settle far away from all the painful memories that he had in New York."

He must have been very old when this was written. I checked the date on the front of the book. May 1960. I continued reading about the house, how he had collected river stone for the porch pillars and fireplace, and chosen the best oak for the stairs and banisters. 'Every board and beam and stone was chosen with Regina in mind,' he had told the author. 'Only the best for her.' And, the author continued, Mr. Stone hinted at secret compartments he had built into the house because his wife had loved little things like that. But, of course he never shared where they were.

He must have been at least 90 or so when the article was written. I returned the magazine to the rack on the librarian's counter. She was checking out a pile of books for a lady, so I waited until she was done.

"Do you know when Mr. Stone passed away, by any chance?" I asked.

She looked at me knowingly. "I don't mean to pry," she said. "But has something happened at that house of yours? Because it won't be the first time, you know."

I was angry for a moment, but realized that the more information I was armed with, the better I could fight whatever it was. "Yes," I said. "Several things. And I am going to get to the bottom of it."

She nodded. She seemed genuinely concerned. "He passed away not long after that article was written, probably about a year or so. He was 91 years old. But he had become senile and was standing on the porch of that house and running people off with his shotgun. Even the mailman stuck the mail in the box as quickly as possible and drove off.

"Mr. Stone must have quit going to the grocery store weeks before he died. Everyone was afraid to check on him, afraid they'd get shot. When they finally found him, after the mailman reported that his box was stuffed full, he was quite decomposed. The only thing in the cabinets was a few stale crackers, and everything in the refrigerator had molded and gone bad. It was a sad situation."

I was horrified. No wonder he haunted the place. What a horrible way to die! "How did you know where I lived?" I asked the librarian.

"Oh, everyone knows when someone new moves into town. Dawson Springs is a very friendly place, and a small place. You can't help but notice. And, besides that, you are not the first person to come looking for information about that house."

"Oh." I was taken aback. "Can you tell me about some of the others?"

"Well, I don't like to gossip. But let's just say that no one has lived in that house for more than a year. A bad atmosphere…and noises, especially gunshots have been heard. Please be careful, dear. There most certainly is something there. I'm not a believer in ghosts myself, but certain conditions can make for an unpleasant feeling in some places that have seen extreme emotion or tragedy."

I took a deep breath. "Well, thank you, Mrs. Bunch. You've been very helpful." I gathered up Sandy and the books he wanted to check out. As I was leaving, I asked if she knew where Mr. Stone was buried.

"Oh, yes, in Rosedale Cemetery, right up front. It's out on Industrial Drive." I thanked her again and we left.

I was excited about the secret compartments, and resolved to look for them right away. Maybe if I could find some of them, they would give me a clue as to why Mr. Stone was hanging around.

Before heading home, I drove out to the big cemetery and along the front row of tombstones. Soon I came to Mr. Stone's grave. The stone was very simple, with only his name, date of birth, and date of death on it. Since he had no family, he must have either left instructions for a very simple stone, or someone had provided it out of the goodness of their heart.

I got out and walked around to the other side while Sandy waited in his booster seat. There was a carving on the other side. Inside of a carved square marked with the directions of North, East, South, and West in that order clockwise, were the words Faith, Hope, Loyalty, and Love, with each one representing a different direction. Faith was at the top (North), Hope on the East side, Loyalty on the South side, and Love on the West side. Very unusual, I thought. He must have planned it himself long before he died, and whatever it represented died with him.

I looked at my watch. It was past lunch time. Sandy immediately began to complain that he was hungry. "Ok, ok, we're going now. How about a hamburger?"

He nodded happily. I swung by the local DQ and picked up a

kids' meal and a cheeseburger for myself and we went home and ate on the back porch. Looking out across the beautiful vista, the fields spread out in the sunshine, the ribbon of highway below, and the river beside it made me appreciate the place more than ever.

I was determined to solve the mystery and get our peaceful life back.

Nothing happened that night. I let Sandy sleep with me as promised. The next morning I was up early and right after we had breakfast, I started a systematic search of the house to try and find the secret compartments. Now, where would I hide them if it were me?

I tapped along the walls, trying to discover if there was a place that sounded hollow. I also felt all along the door panels and facings, tried to move the newel posts on the stairs. Nothing. I looked in the back of closets for hidden panels or doors.

The fireplace in the living room seemed a likely candidate, but as far as I could tell, it was as solid as could be. I tried to move every river rock on it but they were cemented in firmly. I even craned my neck to look up in the chimney, but it was too dark to make out anything. I remembered that the fireplace was decorative, not usable for fires, so it was naturally capped off at the top.

Sandy followed me from room to room with his little car, making vroom vroom noises. At last I grew tired and we went out onto the porch, where he proceeded to run the car along the banister and up the wooden part of the porch posts.

I stood at the edge of the porch and laid my hand up the side of one of the posts. Then it hit me. The posts! Maybe that was it! I took a critical look all around each one. They looked solid enough. I stood back and studied them.

If each side was a panel, then they must be hollow inside. I walked around studying them intently. I placed my thumb on the edge of one of the sides and pulled. Then I pushed. I did it on all four sides of the first post. Then I did the same on the second post. Nothing. The same for the third post. But on the fourth post, I felt something give. I tugged harder. I could see a small gap between the panel I was pulling on and the next.

But I couldn't get it open. It was probably just a place where time and the weather had taken their toll. I sighed.

Greg would be home this afternoon. I had not prepared a bite of supper, or even thought about it. Hurriedly, I rushed in to the kitchen and pulled chicken breasts out of the freezer. The package said you could bake them without thawing. Good. I put them in the pan and covered them in olive oil. I would sprinkle garlic powder and chop up some fresh basil on them just before they got done. Some frozen broccoli and baked potatoes would complete the simple meal.

It was almost 4:00. Once the table was set and I had the chicken and potatoes baking, I opened a can of chicken and stars soup for Sandy and heated it in a pan on the stove. But I couldn't stop thinking about the mystery.

Then another idea came to me. What if the square on the gravestone had something to do with it? And what did it mean if it did?

Where was the clue?

I got out a pad and pen and drew the square on the gravestone as I remembered it. Faith, Hope, Loyalty, and Love. Mr. Stone must have been a more optimistic person in his earlier years. But what did the directions have to do with these words? Could it be he was pointing to something else? I thought about the area around the house.

What was north of the house? In my mind's eye I traveled up Highway 62. The first thing I noticed was the General Baptist Church. Faith...that was it! Now I was excited. Hope...to the east on the road we lived on was an animal shelter—a no kill shelter, at that. They were certainly a place of hope.

South was Loyalty...Just out of town in a southerly direction was what? I thought and thought. Then it came to me. The Masonic Lodge on Highway 109. Wasn't one of their tenets loyalty? So what was Love? It had to be to the west.

But for the life of me I couldn't think of anything but miles of rolling highway to the west. So what did Mr. Stone love? His home, his land, his wife...his wife! He loved his wife so much he could not bear to live in the place where she died. But there were no cemeteries to the west. Besides, she was undoubtedly buried in New York. I shook my head. This would take some figuring out.

I heard Greg's SUV drive in to the driveway, so I took a quick look at the chicken breasts. Just a few more minutes. Sandy flew to the door ahead of me and, after unlocking the door, we practically threw ourselves into Greg's arms.

"Daddy! Daddy!" Greg lifted Sandy up, gave him a kiss, and hugged me fiercely.

"We have missed you so much!" I said, and burst into tears.

"Oh, my dear Sarah! I have missed you so much as well! What on earth is the matter?" He set Sandy down, and wrapped me in his arms.

"I don't know, it's just this prowler and everything, I guess."

"You did get the locks changed, right?"

"Yes, but..." I was afraid to tell him I was now an official believer in ghosts. "We'll talk after supper. It's almost ready. Come on in the kitchen and I'll fix you something to drink."

Greg was soon settled at the table with Sandy on his knee, which was substituting for a galloping horse. I set a glass of iced tea in front of him. He was the best sight I had seen in days.

He helped me with the dishes afterwards and before I forgot it, I gave him his new key. Then we retired to the back porch with more tea and the beautiful river view.

Sandy ran down into the yard with his little car. "Now, what has you so upset, Honey?" Greg asked.

I told him everything that had happened since we talked, and all about what I had learned about Mr. Stone and the house, and also what I suspected were clues on the gravestone. "I know you think I'm crazy, but there is something that is keeping him hanging on here."

Greg looked at me a long time. Then he nodded. "So what do you think we need to do?"

"I think we need to keep looking for what the clues mean." I told him as much as I had figured out, if I was right. "And, if I'm right, I think the west side clue, love, may be the most important one of all."

"I won't say I don't believe you," said Greg. "My grandmother used to tell some stories about things that happened to her, and I know she wouldn't lie."

Greg tried to get Sandy to sleep in his own room that night, but nothing doing. He got right in between us and burrowed into the blankets. I sighed.

"After we get this thing solved...." I said, looking into Greg's eyes. His warm smile just melted me.

"And I will look forward to that," he said.

That night, the shotgun blast sounded like it was right in the room with us. All three of us shot up in the bed.

"What the hell..." growled Greg. He jumped out of bed in his pajamas and raced for the stairs. I grabbed Sandy and was right behind him.

When we reached the front door and Greg flung it open, there was nothing. The night was quiet, only crickets singing and the scent of the magnolia blossoms in the air.

"That is what I've been talking about," I whispered.

"Holy crap," said Greg.

He looked all along the porch. Then he pointed at the post on the west side. "Look!"

One side of it was lying on the porch, splintered. My hand flew to my mouth as we cautiously made our way over to it.

Inside the post was a space, and sitting there was an old urn of some kind, tucked away inside. Greg gingerly took it out. "We need some light."

We took the urn with us back into the house, and to the kitchen. Greg set it on the table and turned on the kitchen light. The urn appeared to be cast iron, with curliqued handles. It was gracefully shaped, with angel wings molded into it on one side, and an engraving on the other. I got an old kitchen towel and wiped away the dirt.

I could now make out the writing on it: Regina, Beloved Wife.

I gasped. "It's his wife's ashes!"

"Well, I'll be," said Greg. "It must have been in there the whole time, from when he built the house. How about that? I'm surprised no one else has discovered it."

We took the urn in and set it on the mantle in the living room after we had cleaned off the grime. "How sad that he never told anyone she was here," I said. Then I realized that that was what he had been trying to do all along!. "Greg?"

He was looking through the newspapers on the coffee table. "Hmm?"

"What side of the house was that post on where the urn was?"

He looked quizzically at me. "The west side, I think. Why?"

"Remember I told you about the square on the tombstone? Love was on the west side! It was a clue. He loved Regina, and her ashes were in the western post! And when we were too dense to find them, he just blasted the side of the post off with his shotgun!"

Greg nodded. "Makes sense. But now what do we do?"

"I think I know exactly what will stop this haunting." And I picked up the phone to call the sheriff.

A few days later, we and a few other people from town, along with Sheriff Thornton stood beside Jeremiah Stone's grave where Regina's ashes had just been interred on top. The undertaker read some scripture, most notably 1 Corinthians 13:4-13. It was all about love. It was a perfect ending to Mr. and Mrs. Stone's story.

I dropped a red rose on the grave when the service was finished.

From that time on, there were no more ghosts, gunshots, or nasty messages. Our house had a tranquil, peaceful feeling. Sandy received a yellow Labrador puppy the next week and the two are now inseparable. I no longer feel nervous or anxious when Greg is away from home.

"And now these three remain: faith, hope, and love. But the greatest of these is love."

VOICES FROM THE PAST

Laura was rushing around trying to get things ready for her part in the summer festival being held in Dawson Springs. She was in charge of a "meet and greet" in the local cemetery. She had all her character volunteers, and they would portray historical people in the town who were buried in the cemetery. Each one would give a talk about his or her life and times.

Her friend Charles Jackson was playing the part of W.I. Hamby, who discovered the mineral wells that led to Dawson Springs becoming a famous spa in the late 1800's and early 1900's. Other townspeople played other characters, such as Dr. A.G Darby, and Theodore Clark, who was the first druggist, along with his partner, George M. Price. The minister of the First Christian Church, Hank Hickman, was going to be J.E. Hayes, who owned the town's only department store in 1902. Another character was Mr. Dennie Clark, who had owned an undertaking business. Lee O. Dixon, who operated a boarding house, and also organized the Dawson Springs Silver Coronet band, was played by Mayor Judy Ross's husband Stanley. Mr. Dixon's descendants were still a part of the community. So Laura had tried to pick someone who not only could act, but resembled Mr. Dixon closely. After the "ghosts" gave their talks, box suppers would be eaten in the cemetery shelter, where card tables and chairs had been set out earlier in the day by the Dawson Springs Ladies' Garden Club. They had also provided pots of summer flowers for decoration.

It looked to be a very festive and informative evening.

Laura had dug deeply for her historical facts, hoping they were all correct, because there was not a lot of material. She shrugged. Oh, well, it was mainly for entertainment, but she hoped people would go away with a better sense of what the town meant, and be proud of their rich history.

She and her friend Sonya had found all the graves and this afternoon they would finish preparing them with folding chairs for the "ghosts" and making sure the wi fi worked for their microphones. The idea was for the narrator, Mayor Judy Ross, to introduce each speaker, and then he or she would rise up from behind the gravestone and begin to talk about his or her life.

"Hey," said Sonya, as she straightened up from a stack of programs that would introduce the players and tell a little about each actor. On one side was a map of the planned talks throughout the cemetery, numbered accordingly. "What time do you and I need to be out there?"

Laura looked at her watch. "I'd say about 5:00, so we can show each actor where to stand and make sure their mikes are working. They are supposed to arrive at 5:15, then we will start the talks with W.I. Hamby at 6."

"But right now we need to take the folding chairs out there. Charles loaded them in the back of his pickup for me. It's parked out back of the shop."

Laura owned a beauty shop in town, and was very active in civic affairs. Her friend Charles worked for the Dawson Salts and Mineral Company, which had revived some of the old wells and was selling the mineral water in green glass bottles. They had a big stake in making the town attractive to tourists.

Sonya grabbed the stack of programs. "I'll just stick these in the truck; then we won't forget them later. I am so excited about this! You know, other towns have had this for years. It is always a big draw. Something about being in a cemetery at dusk, I guess. Did you line up the box suppers?"

"I sure did," answered Laura The IGA deli called a few minutes ago and said we can pick them up anytime." The box suppers, which cost guests $5 each, contained chicken salad sandwiches, a bag of chips, a brownie, and a soft drink. The drinks were iced down already at the IGA and Charles would help her to load them and the suppers into the truck later.

About that time, Mayor Judy Ross came flying in the front door. "Laura! Laura! We have a problem," she said breathlessly.

Sonya groaned softly. That was all they needed.

"What is it, Mayor?" Laura asked.

"Well, the power line we are using out at the cemetery for the spotlights on the actors has gone out. And there is not a big enough one to be found anywhere!" She actually wrung her hands.

Laura frowned. What would they do without lights? 'Duh,' she thought. "Well, we can just use a big flashlight. That'll make it more creepy and true to life anyway. I have 2 or three here some-where. And extra batteries."

Mayor Ross smiled. "Bless you!" And she was gone.

The spotlight type flashlight would be perfect. "It will illumi-nate just enough that it will be hard to recognize the speakers, and they will seem more like their characters," said Laura. "I'll just walk along and shine the light on whoever is speaking."

"Sounds great," said Sonya.

The girls hurried out to the cemetery, driving around to the dif-ferent graves and setting out the chairs. The microphones would be clipped onto the actors' clothing and tested with Laura's laptop.

When they were satisfied that all was ready, they left to go get some lunch. Just before time for the event, they picked up the food and drinks from the IGA, and delivered it to the shelter in the mid-dle of the cemetery, where members of the Garden Club would pass them out.

Laura, Sonya, and the mayor drove the actors around to their graves in a golf cart, left them studying their scripts, and went back to the first grave on the agenda, that of W. I. Hamby. Charles looked magnificent in his old fashioned suit coat, collar, bow tie, and porkpie hat. He had even grown a small mustache for the oc-casion.

"Nervous?" Laura smiled at him.

"A little. But I've been practicing every day, and I think I'll do all right," answered Charles.

By 6 p.m. a large crowd had gathered in the cemetery, showed their tickets, and were milling around W.I. Hamby's grave, waiting for him to speak to them.

Mayor Judy Ross stepped up to where Laura's laptop lay open on a wide gravestone, picked up her microphone, and began to speak. "Welcome, ladies and gentlemen," she intoned. "We are here this evening to pay tribute and learn from some of our more prominent citizens of Dawson Springs' past. We hope you will enjoy our little reenactment, and not be too frightened as the ghostly voices of bygone years regale us with their tales. After we have visited the last grave, which is that of"-- she adjusted her glasses and referred to her program—Mr. Lee O. Dixon, we will have our previously purchased repast in the shelter. We will begin with the voice of Mr. W.I. Hamby."

Sonya stifled a giggle. "She can make anything sound pompous."

Laura smiled. "She is a little dramatic, but that actually fits in quite well with what we're doing tonight."

Then they turned their attention to the gravestone, where Charles appeared to rise up from behind, as Laura shone her light on him. He began to tell how he had first come to Dawson Springs, about his family, and how the mineral water was discovered. He was quite convincing.

When Charles sat back down in his folding chair, the mayor led the crowd down the lane to the next grave. Laura followed, carrying the laptop, making sure the mayor's mike was working correctly and was loud enough.

"Next, we will hear from Dr. A.G. Darby, owner and operator of one of our most popular boarding houses, as well as the first doctor in town."

The sun began to set as "Dr. Darby" began his talk, once again about how he had come to Dawson Springs, and combined two careers with the help of his wife and family.

Laura glanced around the rapidly darkening cemetery. The flashlight gave just the right amount of other worldly light. It was perfect!

Next was Theodore W. Clark and George M. Price, his partner in the first drug business. Since they were not, of course, buried side by side, Laura, Sonya, and Mayor Ross had figured out how to present them together. They decided that Mr. Price had wandered over from his grave to visit Mr. Clark. The audience got a big laugh when he announced this fact. They went on to tell their stories, in the same vein as the others.

J.E. Hayes, owner of the town's first department store, was next, followed by Mr. Dennie Clark, an undertaker. He also got a big laugh with his story about how much he loved baseball, and how one day, as he was leading a funeral procession through town, he stopped in front of the J.E. Hayes Department Store to ask someone what the score was. Back in those days before radio, the downtown businessmen would pay a runner to bring each innings' scores from the depot and post them in the department store window. Someone told him the score, and the funeral procession continued.

The cemetery was really dark now, and some people pulled out small flashlights. "Be careful, watch your step," cautioned the mayor as she led the way to Mr. Lee O. Dixon's grave.

"Lee O. Dixon" rose from his folding chair and delivered an interesting discourse on his different endeavors in the city, and how he helped organize the Dawson Springs Silver Coronet Band. "Many young ladies' hearts were set aflutter by our coronet and trombone players," he said, wiggling his eyebrows and winking, to the delight of the crowd.

Laura's arm was getting tired of holding the big flashlight. She was glad this was the last one. About that time, the flashlight went out! It was very dark, in spite of the smaller flashlights the guests were holding. To "Lee's" credit, he finished his talk, bowed, and sat down.

They had now reached the oldest part of the cemetery. Before Laura could even shake the flashlight, and before the applause had died away, a cold blue light began to glow behind a nearby grave. Everyone turned toward it, surprised.

Sonya and Laura looked at each other, then at the mayor, whose expression could not be read in the dark. "I thought Lee was the last one," whispered Sonya.

"He was. So what is this?"

A voice began to speak, a voice that sounded so eerie and sepulchral that it gave Laura goosebumps. "Good evening, ladies and gentlemen," said the thin, very pale man who stood in the bluish light. He had on a high celluloid collar and tie, a dark suit, and his hair was parted in the middle. "My name is Herschel Alexander. My body was brought home to Dawson Springs from Arkansas in 1904. The other cemeteries in the area were full. My parents were distraught. My father, Jonas "Bush" Alexander, had a large plot of ground and decided to deed it to the town for a cemetery. They reserved enough lots for themselves and the rest of our family. I was the first person to be buried here at Rosedale. I think that is an important thing to know. As you can see," he swept his arm out expansively, "I have a lot of company these days. I do hope you will all come to visit again, as there are many more prominent people here who would like for their stories to be told. Thank you."

And he did not sit down, but appeared to vanish into thin air. Everyone started to oooh and aah, saying how clever that was, and how did they do the lighting, etc. Then the applause was deafening. Laura was able to get the flashlight back on, and when she shined it on the mayor so she could direct people to the shelter for their box suppers, she was surprised to find the mayor pale as a sheet. She had a stunned look on her face. She looked over at Laura and Sonya, whose mouths were still open. Then with a visible effort, she gathered her wits about her and said, "Thank you ladies and gentlemen. Your repast awaits you in the pavilion."

As the crowd began moving away, Laura and Sonya rushed over to the grave. Sure enough, the name on it said "Herschel Alexander." There was no folding chair.

"Well, the mayor is a good actress. I guess she planned this little surprise for us. She looked as shaken as the rest of us," said Laura.

The mayor walked over just them. "Oh, Laura, you and Sonya have outdone yourselves! That last one, well, it really scared me for a bit. That was brilliant, how on earth did you do it? And who was the actor? Not anyone I recognized."

"You mean you didn't do it yourself, Mayor?" asked Laura.

"Why, no, I just assumed…" she trailed off.

They looked back at the grave. The rest of the crowd had already gotten to the lighted shelter in the middle of the cemetery. As one, they all took off at a fast walk.

Later that night, as they were clearing the shelter of tables and chairs with the help of the other actors, Sonya said, "The first person buried here! How could we have left him out?"

Laura smiled. "It looks like he was determined not to be left out. And he is right. There are plenty of people here whose stories need to be told. Looks like this will be a yearly event. And who knows, we might hear from someone else we didn't think of!"

Sonya shuddered. "I hope not!" she said.

Many people asked later how the illusion was done. "It looked just like a real ghost!" exclaimed an old lady whose hair Laura was doing. "Why, even the mayor seemed frightened. I hope there's a surprise character again next year!"

"I hope so, too," said Laura. "The person or persons who concocted the appearance has yet to come forward." She knew in her heart of hearts, however, that no one would be coming forward at all. That is, until next year's surprise ghost appeared.

ABOUT THE AUTHOR

Rebecca Solomon lives with her husband, Mark, and their spoiled cat, Ana, in western Kentucky. She enjoys reading, scrapbooking, and volunteering.

Made in the USA
Charleston, SC
13 October 2016